70% ACRYLIC
30% WOOL

Viola Di Grado

70% ACRYLIC
30% WOOL

*Translated from the Italian
by Michael Reynolds*

Europa
editions

Europa Editions
214 West 29th Street
New York, N.Y. 10001
www.europaeditions.com
info@europaeditions.com

Translation by Michael Reynolds
Original title: *Settanta acrilico trenta lana*
Translation copyright © 2012 by Europa Editions

Library of Congress Cataloging in Publication Data is available
ISBN 978-1-60945-077-9

Di Grado, Viola
70% Acrylic 30% Wool

Book design by Emanuele Ragnisco
www.mekkanografici.com

Cover photo © Merton Gauster/Getty Images

Prepress by Grafica Punto Print – Rome

Printed in the USA

To someone Else

One day it was still December. Especially in Leeds, where winter has been underway for such a long time that nobody is old enough to have seen what came before. It snowed all day, except for a brief autumnal parenthesis in August that stirred the leaves a little and then went back to whence it had come, like a warm-up band before the headliner.

In Leeds anything that is not winter is a warm-up band that screams itself hoarse for two minutes and then dies. Then come the dramatic snowstorms that beat the ground like curses and conspire against the reckless lyricism of the tiny fuchsias blossoming in the park. Give them a round of applause! Encore.

Leeds winters are terribly self-absorbed; each one wants to be colder than its predecessor and purports to be the last winter ever. It unleashes a lethal wind full of the short sharp vowels of northern Englishmen but even harsher, and anyway, neither one of them speaks to me.

To think that it's not winter people fear, but the inferno, in all its fiery warmth. I'd gladly swap one for the other, winter for inferno, if life could be managed like one of my Chinese exercises.

On the rare occasions that I left the house, an icy muzzle immobilized my jaw and the wind whipped my umbrella inside out, tore it from my hands, dragged it meters down the road, and dumped it crippled in the gutter, its ribs up in the air like broken legs. And yet the English persisted in going out in their short trousers and cotton blazers, their shoes and mouths open, wearing the same wide smiles as they had in August, with the same long strides, the same relaxed way of chatting with each other, drawing the syllables out in their mouths, delivering them without haste to the freezing air where they were transformed into steam. Naturally, their umbrellas never broke.

That December day, just back from an exhausting bout of shopping on Briggate, I threw my brand new magenta jacket into a dumpster on Christopher Road.

That's the street I live on, one of those streets whose whereabouts you always have to explain to people, and even you can never be sure where it is because it's identical to the street before it and the one after, and also because the second you get to Christopher Road denial of its sheer ugliness pushes you onward. It's so ugly, Christopher Road is, that it qualifies as proof of God's nonexistence. Its gaunt red-brick houses to start with, each one the same as the last, each one with its black metal door like the doors of isolation cells; then the bags of garbage tossed out beside wheelies; the sweeping panorama over the takeaways on Woodhouse Street, which crosses Christopher Road, though no street in its right mind would ever choose to do so.

To the right you can admire Tom's £3-only fish & chip shop, and feast your eyes on neon-blazoned kebab shops. To the left, there's Nino's one-quid pizza slices, and down the road, chicken and bamboo shoots or fried seaweed at the Chinese all-nighter.

Then there's that opening-credits darkness, like when you're sitting in the cinema, anxiously waiting for a movie to start. But on Christopher Road nothing ever starts. If anything, it ends. Everything ends, even things that have never started. Food, for instance, goes bad even before you open it, because there are blackouts all the time; flowers die before they've bloomed because there's no sun; fetuses have a naughty habit of strangling themselves with the placenta.

It was originally a workers' village. The factory was the center of the town, then came the workers' houses, and then the church. Everything was built with an eye to saving money on materials and aesthetics, and since it cost less, all the houses went up instead of out, every one of them three narrow stories high, like so many droll towers of Babel to get to the devil. The factory is an elementary school now. When the bell rings, it releases hoards of baby bag-snatchers into the streets.

The church, on the other hand, is still a church. Tall and dark, its gothic head watches over the flock of headstones. But I'm the only one who ever goes there—it's been deconsecrated, and the deceased are forgotten to the world. I go there to spy on the dreams of the dead, and to lop the tops off of flowers that sprout there by mistake. No one brings them there to honor anybody's memory. In fact, remembering is strictly forbidden: thornbush extends like wrinkles over the headstones to hide the names.

But sometimes, despite everything, I find flowers underfoot as I make my way between the weeds, the thornbushes, and the slumbering snakes. There! A small stain of innocent baby blue resting in the scrub's old-lady hands, a splash of beauty in that spin-dryer of misery and death. A provocation is what it is, and *snip*, like the fairy that nobody dares invite to the fairytale party I cut it off without mercy.

Then I return home.

You're thinking that Christopher Road is the last place to set a novel, let alone the story of one's life, but looking at it now on the page, I see myself there clear as anything, like in a school pic.

I'm the one with the big nose and the long black hair. My complexion lighter than light. No, further over there, to the right, I mean the one with the bangs and the green eyes. Can you see me or not? The one rummaging in a dumpster, yeah, there.

The story of my life? Hardly. My life has no story; it has distortions in place of stories. Deep craters full of sand where stories should be, that's what my life has, like the ones on the moon, the ones that looked like eyes, nose, and a mouth when you were a kid.

Zoom in on me, dark-haired with bangs, as I toss my magenta jacket. Snow had transformed the shopping bags into twee little snowmen. And right at that moment, as I was shoving my jacket into the dumpster, I saw a dress. A crumpled forest green dress with white buttons poking out from under a plastic Sainsbury's bag. One long sleeve extended like a green snake over a little yellow plastic stool on the right. On the left it didn't have a sleeve.

It made me think of one afternoon so long ago and so different from that day that remembering it was like inventing it all over again. My mother is studying the label of a black sweater with rhinestones, because back then she still bought clothes. We're at the White Rose Shopping Center, it's raining outside, and, all excited, I'm telling her about my first Chinese lesson.

"And there are tones! Isn't it absurd? I mean, depending on the tone you use, the word '*ma*' can mean 'mummy,' or 'insult,' or 'horse,' or 'cannabis!'"

"Can you read what's on the label, dear? It's so small."

And, concentrating on the hieroglyphic of the basin with the hand inside it, I go: "Hand wash."

"No, I mean the fabric."

"100% angora."

"Oh really! I'm going to try it on."

"What about this one?"

She grabs the white turtleneck sweater and turns the collar out: "Why, no, dear. 70% acrylic."

I fished the green dress out of the dumpster. It was long, large, made of coarse cotton and as shapeless as a garbage bag. It had a high-buttoned neck, and the top three buttons skewed to the right and were stitched with a different kind of thread. The neck was clearly too tight. I put it in my bag. Then I noticed another dress that had been hiding beneath the one I'd taken. It was red, made of heavy wool. It, too, had only one very long sleeve and a plunging neckline that ran all the way down to the navel. The fitted bust darts were clearly too high, and pointy, as if they had been made not for breasts but for those pyramids they put on desks supposedly to improve your memory. I took that one as well.

Wait! This moment must have a name, so I can call it like a dog and it will come running back to me. I will call it the start of year zero.

So, before that came year minus one.

Before that minus two.

Before that minus three.

Stop counting at minus three because that's when my father dies.

When I came in, my mother was on her knees next to the kitchen table, in her underwear, intent on photographing a hole that the woodworms had left in our table.

I stared at her taut leg muscles and the cruel razor's edge of her spine. I watched her body—an old and haggard body that records showed had been alive for forty-six years. The bones of her rickety back moved as she adjusted the composition of her shot. They were present and alert; they were beasts ready to pounce, those bones. They were oracles of premature death by deterioration. They protruded from her flaccid excuse for skin, a pallid, almost transparent veil darkened here and there by bruises that she got when she fell out of bed. Even her periods had stopped some months ago. She was done. My mother was ready to be, in a word, thrown away. Yes, I know, that's two words, but it's better that way: one for her and one for me, because if I have to throw her away, I won't be far behind.

"C'mon, Mamma, no more pictures. I'm going to get the meat ready."

She turned to face me and said the look: *Why won't you let me take a photo of the hole?*

I replied with the look: *Because it's a stupid waste of time and it's not doing you any good, obviously.*

Her hair had been dirty for too long. Her large, scanty eyebrows cast a gloomy shadow over her eyelids. Her eyes bulged out of her wan face like large, pearl-white snail shells. The color from her irises was nothing but a tiny detail in the milky bowl of her eyeballs. Yes, the eyes are the mirror of the soul, but by then my mother's soul was far from being vain enough to want to gaze into any mirror.

Standing there with her eyes downcast, she let me put the camera away in its faux leather carrier pouch. I went into the kitchen, pulled the scaloppini out of the freezer, and put them in the microwave. I watched the blood frothing and bubbling up from the pieces of meat as they turned round and round like vital organs that had bravely fled a body somewhere and were now intent on their celebratory ring-around-the-rosy.

A flash popped in the living room.

I emptied the packet of spices onto our cutlets and arranged them on plates; I cut hers into tiny pieces, smaller and smaller until I had sated my homicidal urges, and I opened the fridge to get some water. There was nothing there but a bottle of my father's Heineken, which had become a Disneyland of strange brown organisms. If I watched them without batting an eyelid, they moved. I threw the bottle into the bin.

I pulled it out again.

I put it back in the fridge, between the transparent container where we used to keep the Italian cheeses, now carpeted in mold, and the empty blue-plastic heart where we used to put the lettuce, washed and cut. They say you can tell everything about a family from its fridge.

Anyway, the mold was even thicker there.

In the empty heart, I mean.

My mother ate her scaloppini the way tigers eat in documentaries, burped, and wiped her mouth. She lifted her thin face etched with a complete London underground map of wrinkles, picked up her Polaroid camera from the table, and walked off.

Noise from the stairs.

Another burp.

"You have been listening to *Casta Diva*, Livia Mega on the flute. Stay with us on Pearl Radio."

Like I'm going to budge from my plate of cold meat.

I had a camera once. And a blue plush penholder. And a photo album. And fifty-nine CDs and sixty-seven DVDs. And a Chinese cookbook, a silver metallic stereo, and a Tweety Bird makeup case, and and and, you can line up ands forever. Those ands I'm always thinking about but that never spare a thought for me, ands that, when you string them together, form a story from which I have been expelled.

I had just moved everything into the apartment on Victoria Road, where I was supposed to live alone and get my degree in Chinese, and believe in the future like any other sane person.

The little yellow lights on the mirror.

The porcelain geisha in a flower-print kimono on the bedside table.

Puccini and Verdi, gifts from my mother, and the entire Björk collection arranged in alphabetical order in the top drawer.

The red and green Indian rug. Books on Taoism and yellowing editions of fairytales from when I lived in Turin on Via Vanchiglia.

A leather photo album in which I grew older every time you

turned a page: at age six, in Piazza Castello, Turin; at age seven, upon arrival in Leeds; and, a few minutes later, I'm eighteen again, sitting in an old flat on Victoria Road with three months of lessons behind me, many more ahead, and a bunch of empty pages to fill with photos.

I love photo albums. They convince you that time moves forward, like when you're in the car and the trees out the window look like they're moving backwards.

But then I never went to live on Victoria Road. On December twelfth, while I was hanging a poster of my favorite singer over the bed, my mobile rang. I picked it up from the windowsill. The window opened onto a fake sun, a splatter of egg yolk on the sick white of the sky.

I remember the people talking and walking outside, I remember every one of them. I remember the triumphant way they strolled hand in hand, the wholesomeness of their faces, their pink lips, unchapped by the cold, stretched wide in supercilious smiles like a virgin bride's bloodstained sheets.

I remember the freshly painted façade of the Headingley Office Park, too.

I answered the call and my mother was crying. "Something's happened," she said between sobs.

"What, Mamma? What?"

"Come to the hospital. Now."

"Mamma, what's happened?!"

"Your father."

Down there the people were still smiling. What a waste of facial contractions when they could have just as easily pelted me with stones.

Björk stayed where she was with her face dangling, one thumbtack in, and three to go. Doubtless, when I left, she fell like a corpse onto the mattress. In fact, she never returned to my lips when I was under the shower, where once upon a time I used to sing her at the top of my voice.

It was eleven-o-five, my last eleven-o-five, because I left my diver's watch in the flat with everything else. The car sped toward the hospital and the road unraveled before me like thread off a bobbin, trees houses takeaways homeless people florists banks, there were *sapiens Homo sapiens* everywhere and worse still the sun was out, protecting them all. Each thing sailed along with ease, blended joyfully with every other thing, like in one of those American movies with the hottest actors who, in the end, learn the importance of inner beauty, maybe even to the sound of the latest hit by some anorexic pop star. "Come to the hospital," my mother had said. "Now." Whenever she spoke she gave the impression of leaving something out; you felt the heft of a word hidden beneath the others. Always. I hated it. Verbal tumors that needed to be cut out with a scalpel lest they turn into facts.

She wasn't at the hospital. When he stopped breathing I went to look for her at home. She was standing in front of the door, the key held tight in her fist. I watched her from behind, her shining blond hair, her severe shoulders, her thin body draped in a turquoise two-piece suit.

"Mamma."

Her face turning towards mine, drawing me into the excruciating pale-blue universe of her eyes. Her perfect beauty. Her conclusive beauty.

"Mamma."

The sky is just a low-cost remake of her eyes. The sun is a low-cost remake of her hair. I am a low-cost remake of her genes.

I took a step towards her.

"I can't do it."

"Do what, Mamma?"

"Open the door."

I took the key from her hand. It was warm with sweat and smelled of metal. Of course keys smell of metal. Except those plastic ones that babies play with. I pushed on the key and turned it in the lock. Twice. Three times. Then our old pitch-black door moaned and let itself be opened. My mother went in. I stopped and turned to look at the city, which stayed outside, and I realized that it, too, was dying. The sky was pale and withered like a terminal patient. I closed my eyes and begged for cosmic euthanasia.

At some point there's a moment. A moment gift wrapped especially for depressives. A moment of unbridled instinct for survival in which you are tired of being the only stationary object in this turbine-drunk-on-will of a universe.

If this were a love story, that moment would have occurred upon me meeting a blond Englishman to the sound of a string quartet playing softly in the background. But this is not a love story, however much it would like to be. It would sacrifice ten whole paragraphs to be a love story, or surrender a character, and if that didn't do it, throw in two lines from every dialogue, but that's enough already, enough of this begging, nobody would ever adopt it as a love story, everyone knows that mongrel pups imploring you to love them from a cardboard box on the street never get taken home. Even those people with Leeds Dog Care Society pins on their lapels stop, say, "How cute," and move on.

Anyway, my moment was in December of the year zero, that is, two thousand and seven, the day of the magenta jacket. I had woken up during the night to my mother's respiratory concerto. She was sleeping outside my door, in a fetal position. What by day was the most negligible inhaling and exhaling, by night took on a sort of prehistoric carnality that could not be ignored.

I sat down next to her.

I spoke the look, *Go up to your room Mamma the floor is cold*. She breathed me a cavernous, *Let me be*.

It must have been seven in the morning but it was dark outside, like at any self-respecting hour of the day in Leeds. They discriminate against daylight hours here, ghettoizing them behind curtains.

There! I was leaning over my mother, watching her fall back to sleep, listening to her breathing in two-four time . . . There it was! That moment when your survival instinct is let loose. At moments like these you can hardly remain indifferent. Either you second them with a burst of life, or you wash them away with your blood.

Of course, the survival instinct is the most vulgar of all human instincts. And naturally, like Jesus, I felt a greater pull to crucifixion. But where was I going to find Judeans ready to condemn me and witness my martyrdom with the appropriate gusto? And there can be no martyrdom without an audience. Which is why, in the end, I chose to go shopping instead.

Leeds was immobilized in an orthopedic back brace of snow. There were no more roofs, no lawns, and it was still snowing. The pointed bell towers that in autumn were black witches' nails were now soft and impersonal shapes adrift in the sky.

As for the sun, poor sod, it was an exhausted speck caught somewhere in the bare branches of dying trees.

Leeds is like one of those sadistic pet owners that waves a piece of meat in front of his dog and then gobbles it down himself. You go out and you see that sun hanging from the sky and you feel happy. You think: Maybe the snow will end. You close your eyes hoping to feel warmth against your eyelids, but the sun has already disappeared, leaving the sky opaque and off-white, the color of a raw chicken thigh.

The thing is that Leeds adores scarecrows, things that fob themselves off as other things, so when you fall for the trick the city laughs at you, especially if you're Italian and you have the sun in your genes. Leeds guffaws, each burst of laughter a thunderclap. Even Hyde Park is actually called Woodhouse Moor. People call it Hyde Park to make you think that you're strolling along the much more spacious and luxuriant avenues of Hyde Park, London.

But I'm not fooled. I've figured out the whole scarecrow scam. How could I be duped into thinking that those white beasts surrounding me are houses and post offices and trees and cars camouflaged by the snow, and not the six-headed sentries of my private circle of the inferno? How could I mistake that pallid shrunken sun for a real sun and not the delirious reveries of some morphine-addled terminal patient at St. James Hospital? How could I even begin to think that the English are kind simply because they smile.

I've divined the truth, I have: the English and the sun and the cars buried under all that white and the postmen and the dogs and the hours and the minutes and my pale face in the mirror are nothing more than passing incarnations of death. And seeing how I've figured all this out, you can stop fucking smiling, I barked at the bald postman who was following me.

He replied that there was another letter for me from the Gagliardi washing machine company.

I slipped it into my bag.

Skirting the park, I held my umbrella in front of me like a shield, careful to keep it at right angles to my body. Raising it even a smidgen would result in the wind whipping the canopy off. I tightened my fingers around the handle. My hair and my raincoat were soaked. What a pain.

I turned towards Hyde Park. The sky merged seamlessly with the ground, white on white, a universal conspiracy of whiteness, betrayed only by the black flashes of crows that now and again glided over the grass. But when they dared stop for more than a few seconds, even they risked being trounced by a clump of snow lying in ambush in the crooks of trees. Like some demon drenched without warning by the Holy Spirit, one poor frightened little crow shook off its sudden white coat. I watched it for a couple of minutes as it spread its wings.

There was no hope for anyone or anything.

I passed the kebab sellers and the vintage clothing boutiques, the Parkinson Building, the supermarkets, and all of a sudden I was in the center of town.

Briggate high street was pompous and garish. It couldn't care less about the snow. Nor could the people, who were walking in and out of Starbucks and Borders, McDonald's and the HMV store with nothing special on their minds, making beelines from shop fronts to the pseudo-Italian bars with their fake leather armchairs and long watery pseudo-espressos.

Naturally, even the clothing stores were teeming with people, divided into species like at a zoo. The casual types went to H&M, the ones who felt trendy to Top Shop, the ones who thought they were chic to Zara, and the-main-thing-is-that-it-doesn't-cost-much set to Primark, but anyway it doesn't matter, what's important is that the clothes are covered in glitter, like when you drip some oil on a crust of bread for the family dog.

I ran the gauntlet of shopping-starved hyenas, managing to avoid the salesgirls with their aggressive "Can I help you"s and their Diana-tint manes set afire by the ceiling neons. I slipped between rows of rhinestoned apparel and acrylic sweat tops blazoned with totally invented Chinese characters, and flew past an entire rack of Levi's jeans unchanged from seventy years ago, except for the label "new style."

I was planning on taking refuge in some neutral zone, like the old ladies' underwear-with-bellyband department, but there was no respite to be had there. A couple of aging biddies were waving around pairs of extra-large flesh-colored undergarments and descanting about how the world would be different if Sean Connery had never stopped playing 007. I stole toward the star-studded bras with glittery inlays disguising mighty padding, but one old biddy had locked onto me: "Excuse me, do you have this in a size smaller?"

"I don't work here."

"Oh, sorry."

As I was walking away, she called out again: "And do you have it without the bellyband?" I had made it all the way to casual clothing, but the rickety old hag was following me, like something out of a zombie flick. "Ex*cuuu*se me?"

I gave her the slip, but there were more of them. Too many! And not only old women, there were young people as well. And really young people. There were people everywhere, walking around in pairs, smiling at each other, their hands plunged into piles of discount clothes, pressing their booty to their breasts with ravenous apoplectic joy, looking at themselves in the mirror like animals lusty for blood.

There was nothing for me in that store. All the clothes were too new, too flashy, too clean. The necklines mocked me, and the skirts pitied me. In the dressing room my knobby knees implored me to go back to trousers. All the same, I forced myself to buy a magenta leather jacket, saying over and over that three years earlier I would have liked it.

Precisely! Three years earlier.

I caught the bus home as fast as I could. It was the first bus I had taken for a long time. The commotion I witnessed obliged me to get off, gasping for breath, one stop before mine. It was a Noah's Ark of people in constant movement, as if the motion of the bus weren't enough for them. Of course, people move when they're on the street too, but watching them move about in such a small confined space, they look like insects trapped in a jar, racing around without any purpose at all; you almost expect them to start walking on the ceiling. They go upstairs to look down on the street from above, or they stand up to greet a blond girl who, due to some genetic mystery is their Philosophy of Psychology teacher despite her being clearly still in puberty.

Then they make their way towards the door, each of them tossing out "sorrys" as if they were bargaining chips. Two descending notes to be intoned with the utmost sugariness, softening every gesture, annulling any act along with its motivations.

All you need is sorry and you can look askance for two entire minutes at the Spanish woman sitting in the second row because she doesn't depilate her eyebrows, or you can put a bullet in her head, or, oh I don't know, fuck your London colleague. You say: "Sorry, may I fuck you?" And maybe you use the same word, a passkey word, to tell your wife about it: "Sorry, I only wanted a fuck. That's why I'm dead now, because I wanted to fuck another woman, but so sorry, I'm very sorry, do you hear me?"

I got off at Hyde Park Corner. At home, I saw two kids in short sleeves sitting on the ground in front of my house. They asked me for some money to buy whiskey and I thought of telling them how shit my life was, to further whet their thirst for alcohol, but I kept it short instead and used the more practical "sorry." It's pure genius if you think about it, to abridge entire discourses with a simple disyllable.

But the kids cursed my mother and my grandmother and even the sister I don't have. It was then that I realized I still had the shiny red-polka-dotted shopping bag from the clothes store in my hand. I dropped it like it was some kind of ugly insect. Then I picked it up again. I examined the jacket, the impeccable geometry of the pockets, the proud color of the leather, the thick silver of the buttons. I picked at the top button with my nails. I pulled the next one up by the roots. I put the third in my mouth and after a few chews spat it out. Finally, I gave up. Even the two kids had lost interest by then, though one of them picked up the button I had spat out thinking that it was worth something. I held the jacket in both hands and buried that shameless magenta in the dumpster. And that's when I found the two defective dresses.

I went inside, into our sad tumbledown house on Christopher Road, a few steps from the church with the abandoned cemetery. We have never been poor, but my father had a perverted taste for discarded things; it made him feel less middle-class. It was ironic, because in the end he, my father, was always at the editorial offices, while my mother was always at home with her flute.

There was never anybody on my street. Maybe some kids with sharp accents who had plans to steal your wallet. At night it was worse because even they disappeared. You would have given an arm to see one of them pass by, but there was no one, nothingness, an appalling reminder of the world as it was pre-Big Bang. Our house became a nowhere house, a flimsy raft adrift in the night; with its three narrow floors all drunk on dampness, full of dust and the rotten smells; and its thin walls that threw every tortured cry of the wind and the rain in our faces.

On the ground floor, the floor closest to hell, closest to the holes where the dead decompose and the skeletons that watch us through eye sockets colonized by worms, was the living room, in it a dusty TV that only picked up channel 4, and two bikes that had once been spanking new but whose flat tires now looked melted onto the carpet.

The steep creaky staircase led to a first floor, where I lived, and a top floor, where the room containing my mother's living corpse was.

And that's why sometimes I preferred to turn right and go home to the cemetery.

There were the little lights on the mirror.
There was the geisha on the bedside table.
There was the Indian rug.
There were the books on Taoism from when I lived in Turin on Via Vanchiglia . . . Oh, and the yellowing fairytales, too, which, even when they turn yellow, still live happily ever after.

I had already moved everything into my new house on Victoria Road. That's what you usually do: things go into houses, rugs are walked on by men, fairytales stack their happy endings onto faux wood bookshelves. And that's almost what happened, but then it all fell into holes—things, houses, rugs, and even the princesses eternally kissed for the first time, everything—the minute it struck year three.

December. Two thousand and four. When I write it I fall into the two zeros.

In two thousand and four my father had that London lover and he fell into a ditch.

Of course there's a logical connection between these two things! For example, before entering the ditch that day he had entered Liz Turpey. She moaned in her prissy southern accent. Obviously, I don't know for sure if she moaned; I have a bad habit of imagining things that hurt me. But whether she did or not, the fact is that on December twelfth, two thousand and four, she was in the car with him, and that is not the fruit of my imagination because they found the bodies together, and I was there I tell you.

Her red silk shirt, with the enormous mark across her breast like a sticker on a banana, was still unbuttoned. There's never anybody on those narrow streets anyway. The houses are hidden in the foliage. They seem alone and abandoned, unhappy, and that's what makes them so beautiful.

As for Liz (yes, I know, I've mentioned her often enough now that you're growing fond of her. Next you'll be taking flowers to her grave), her job was to proclaim the CD *X* and the CD *Y* masterpieces of avant-garde innovation; at least that's what *she* thought her job was—publicity, oodles of it, even though nobody had asked her to say nice things about everybody. My father, on the other hand, wrote the city pages and on his desk he had a silver-framed photo of me at age seven. I'm on the beach at Scarborough; it's during our first trip to England;

my face is thin and happy. I got my thin face from my grand-mother and my happiness from the sand, which I grabbed at violently, pulling it up like carrots, roots and all, because I loved to make holes. In fact, in the photo my hands are buried in the sand up to my forearms, and there's sand on my legs too.

On December twelfth, two thousand and four, the two of them turned into Grosvenor Road, a lane so quiet that you feel like you're in the year three thousand inside the National Museum of English Cottages saying, "Yes, but, it's so terribly artificial because back then there were people and dogs and, well, a little life." But you'd be mistaken.

On Grosvenor Road talking is unnatural, words come out mangled, with too many vowels or too many consonants. They reverberate in the air with a shameful weight, scattering extra meanings about, meanings they don't deserve. On Grosvenor Road if you say, "I'm happy," it becomes "I'm happy to be with you." So Liz Turpey probably smiled at my father and said something to him, and no matter what is was that she actually said it became "take me," because every word uttered on Grosvenor Road gets you under somebody's clothes. On Grosvenor Road the heart-shaped cobalt-blue wrought iron gates and the glistening well-kept lawns are there only to high-light the brutal death to come.

My father must have said things he'd never said before, vir-gin words that made no sense beyond Grosvenor Road, not least because far from that lane my mother was playing the flute all day and when he came home at night they exchanged nary a word.

Anyway, he said them, and she said them too, those things, and they did them, too. Then he started the car.

"Careful, the ditch!"

I don't know if she said that.

I don't know if he heard her and instantly stopped thinking of her nipples and his saliva shining on the brown flesh of her areola (there I go imagining things again), nor whether, right before registering the sensation of the car sliding downward, he glimpsed that gaping vagina of dirty earth sucking him down.

I wasn't there.

But god I was there when they found the bodies, the bodies and the blood in the ditch.

His death immediately hit the pages of the newspaper he wrote for, but instead of being in the byline his name appeared in enormous letters at the top of the column. What a strange thing. How weird that your name swells when you stop living, like the flesh of drowned bodies. And how weird to see his round face smiling next to the word "dead." And not just because "dead" is so close to "dad."

They filled the ditch with concrete. But my mother is still down there and I'm the only one who knows. Nature sometimes takes things that don't belong to it. I discovered that when I was seven and was digging holes in the sand at Scarborough. Buried in the sand was a piece of bottle glass that the sea had stolen and turned into a stone.

I kept that strange shiny green pebble in my jewelry case. As for my mother, I kept her in a room that was not hers at the top of the stairs, a room where my father's Simenons and his collection of beer caps were nowhere to be found and his T-shirt with the faded laughing face of John Lennon was not strewn over the chair.

I left my things in the house on Victoria Road because I thought I wouldn't need them anymore. I was right. Six days later the landlady called me—"What do I do with your boxes?" I told her to turf them out. Then I turned off my mobile.

Our vocal cords went into mourning right about that time. My mother gave up talking gradually, like it was a natural and necessary part of the life-cycle.

The snow had only recently begun its work of annihilation

and from the window I watched the houses disappear like memories. It was December becoming January, changing its skin dirtied with dry leaves and mud, becoming as white as a wedding to which we were not invited.

One day, as if nothing out of the ordinary had happened, all that was left of a typical lunchtime sentence, "salt with that," was "salt," like the salt laid upon the breasts of corpses in Scottish funerals. My mother said, "Salt?" in her thin voice, and I knew that I had to preserve that word in my ears like the song of some rare bird. Through the kitchen window I could see the snow slaying the last patch of green in the flower garden. No matter. It was already half dried up anyway, and people always left their rubbish right next to it, and there was all that gray in the middle, like an old man's hair.

My mother joined me at the window. Her eyes held no expression in them, in one hand was the saltshaker, her other hand rested on the glass without making any mark. *Do you want it or not?* No, she didn't say it out loud, but that was the question.

"No, Mamma, I don't want salt. How long has it been since you washed your hair, Mamma?"

Before long other sentences were mutilated, everyday sentences, the kind you think will never change, like, "Good morning," and, "Did you already add sugar?" There, too, only the word "sugar" remained. And then it left as well.

My mother stopped talking, she didn't utter another word.

Which may be another reason why, in the end, January never came.

First I thought that my mother's silence was a punishment she reserved especially for me. But one day the people from Channel 4 arrived—two forty-somethings with the same pool-blue eyes and the same double chin. "So, Mrs. Mega, are you ready for the show at the Grand Theatre?"

Mrs. Mega didn't reply. She was wearing a gray tracksuit

from who knows where. I'd never seen it before. It had a brown mark in the shape of a fish on the chest—it may have been coffee, but it looked more like rust. She sat motionless on our faded sofa, the poppies in the pattern crushed beneath her, like the ones you put between the pages of a book to dry and they end up crushed to death by all those words.

"My mother has not been playing a lot recently."

"Mrs. Mega, would you like us to come back another time for the interview?"

No answer. Only long, empty gazes and gigantic flowers fuzzy with dust beneath her body.

I accompanied the journalists to the door. When I opened it, I discovered an enormous vulgar sun that had been mysteriously regurgitated from some wintery hole and now sat in front of my house like a flea-bitten dog that wants to come in and lick the food on your table.

"No, sorry," I stammered. "It's just that you never see it here in December, the sun I mean."

"Actually, miss, it's March."

The fatter of the two had spoken, and his thin excuse for a mouth had hardly moved, but his double chin doddered theatrically.

"Mind your own fucking business."

The journalists said good-bye coolly. I watched them walk to their car, an awful green, enveloped in the same light as were clumps of snow under my Goofy slippers. How could it be March with all this snow around? They couldn't have been journalists; more likely, those two lunatics had escaped from some asylum. You've got to be careful whom you invite into your house; they might steal an organ, or even worse, offload an orphan.

Orphans are the privileged ones. They use up all of people's pity and don't leave any for the half-orphans. "Half-orphans," that's a nice name for it. Because, you see, apparently I don't even deserve a word to describe myself. At most I get a circumlocution: "orphaned by her father." Wow! They get universal compassion and I get periphrasis. They get a new family and I get my old family halved and gone insane. And they make millions of movies about them, oh sure, people love the trembling hands of Oliver Twist begging for a bowl of soup, but nobody would want to watch me as I feed my mother, or as she throws her plate on the floor, or as I listen to her conclusive belch the way I always used to listen to the final high note of *Casta Diva*.

She used to play at the top of the stairs because the acoustics were good and I would watch her from below. When she finished she waved the head of the flute around sending small drops of liquid flying. Then she would put the three pieces back into the long black carrying case that now resembles nothing if not a coffin in my eyes.

She smiled and came towards me—how beautiful she was, even our horrible house was enslaved to her beauty, obliged to participate in it. The dust hid beneath the furniture, the light concealed the damp stains on the ceiling, the shadows cloaked the hole in the table, and the TV woke two hitherto unseen channels from their hibernation.

A documentary about superintelligent dolphins appeared on BBC 1. They obeyed the orders of their trainer, a pretty girl with blue hair. They leaped, danced, and pirouetted, and there was one who, seated at a computer, wrote essays about Schopenhauer.

Of course she knew that her husband was cheating on her. Of course she was unhappy. Of course she cried at night until she heard his key in the lock and then, out of pride, pretended to be asleep. But even then, when I would come in and her eyes would be puffy from crying and her face ravaged from sobbing, and I would stand there in the doorway and look at her like she was a painting, even then, when she was so sad and with her cheek crushed against the pillow she'd say, "Ciao," she was so beautiful, even then, and so who needed happiness?

No, I didn't try to comfort her, to free her from that unhappiness. When, from her bed, with her long hands pressed over downcast eyes, she said, "Camelia, I know he's got another woman," I merely contemplated her. I stood still at the door, still as the door, annulled by all that beauty I had no right to console.

"I know, I know who it is, it's that woman who writes about music, the redhead, Liz Turpey, are you listening to me, Camelia? Sweetheart, are you listening? What should I do?"

The blue coverlet imitating the shape of her legs and hips, stopping short of her breasts. Light from the rice-paper lampshade that we bought in Chinatown in London falling on Livia Mega's cheeks, imitating their color, but poorly. So, too, the coverlet. Failed attempts all.

"Camelia, why don't you answer me?"

After *Casta Diva* she descended the stairs towards me like a star, ran her hand over my shamefully black head of hair, and said, "Did you like it, dear?"

"Yes, especially the part where the journalists ask you about your projects and you gaze at them like a wax statue at Madame Tussauds, but one that doesn't really look like Mrs. Mega."

Bang.

I slammed the door and shut everything out, the deceptive light, the journalist's car driving away forever, and the cotton-candy-if-you-behave colored sky.

My mother was still on the sofa. "Next time I won't open the door, don't worry," I said.

She answered the look, *I think that's best,* and the stains on her tracksuit moved to the other side, maybe it was a trick of the light, or the dark, what do I know.

"Mamma, where did you get that tracksuit?"

No answer.

*

I had an idea. I took her flute and hid it. Sooner or later she would have to open her mouth to ask me where it was. She'd know it was me. I did it all the time when I was a child. I used to put it in the washing machine any time she was playing too many concerts and not paying enough attention to me. I'd gaze at it for hours with ruthless curiosity. It was like watching a silvery eel through the porthole of a submarine.

I hid it in the washing machine that day, too. It gave me a strange pleasure to take it apart, transforming it into three little metal arms, the defenseless limbs of a robot. I stuck it inside and closed the door.

Two days went by. Then my mother found it by herself. I was sitting in the kitchen trying to figure out why our phone bill had come to a hundred pounds given that we'd lost the cordless. My excogitations amounted to drawing stupid doodles on the bill. Outside through the dirty window there was snow, nothing else. It had swallowed the next-door neighbors' doghouse, which you could usually see from the kitchen, and also the fake sun those two overweight journalists had brought with them.

She materialized in her gray tracksuit, which bore a new sauce stain around the belly, big and red like a rash. Beneath the kitchen light it looked like a Chinese amulet.

She took the flute out of the washing machine and carefully reassembled it. She lifted it to her lips. I watched her as she closed her eyes and pushed down on the keys. But no sound came out. I nearly had a heart attack: maybe the dampness of the washing machine had ruined it. But when she left the kitchen I grabbed it and tried to play, with my heart in my throat. It still worked. Although when I play it, the sound that comes out resembles the whistle of an empty train going around in circles.

December continued with no hitches really, except for the fact that it stubbornly began afresh when it got to the thirty-first. But it was all for the best, who can stand those New Year's Day lunches anyway.

And my mother continued not to talk. Not even when my grandmother called from Italy—a perverse ritual that she inaugurated when I purchased a wall-mounted telephone. I'd say, "Here she is," and hang the receiver back on the wall, where it remained for the duration of the call.

I was confused. One expects people to talk. One expects many things from human beings.

"C'mon, Mamma, let's go out. Please. I'll take you to buy some sheet music."

She replied with her eyes. Like a child behind an aquarium, I observed her obtuse hibernations on the sofa. Lying there supine, she would open and close her eyes, study the ceiling, and then turn on her side and start on the walls.

"Mamma, should I get you some green tea?"

Silence.

I came back with the teacup and she was still lying on her side. She sat up and I sat down next to her. I asked if she wanted more sugar and waited for some kind of reply, a look, or a nod, anything really. Even her breath becoming vapor I found had meaning as smoke signals.

"Mamma, should I call someone to fix the heaters?"

"Do you want more spaghetti?"

"Should I leave this on or put on a DVD?"

Every question came back to me like a boomerang. "This is all wrong," I told her again, and she gazed at the spider climbing on the ceiling. "How are you this morning?" and she closed her eyes. "Do you want your milk warm or cold?" and she went to the bathroom. "That actress has gotten really old, right?" and she bit her nails.

Certain days it seemed she was competing with objects at who could go longer without making noise. She would station herself in front of the fridge and just stand there. She always won.

My voice was a shameful promontory jutting out from her silence.

When a colleague of hers, a violinist, discovered why she had quit playing she said, "You're a fool to throw your life away like that." My grandmother would say the same thing over the telephone, but I would smile. By then, I was part of it, too.

Nobody understood: it's words themselves that are antithetical to life. They're born in your head, you nurse them in your throat, and then you spray your voice all over them and kill them forever. The tongue is a witless crematorium that would like to share but instead destroys, like Edward Scissorhands' blade-fingers that cut when they caress.

I quit talking as if it were a problem with cigarettes. I learned to block my words as one learns to do with other embarrassing bodily noises.

It was that December day on which the pamphlet kid came with his last flier—an ad for a garbage disposal unit. I watched him stick our final brochure in the slot, I watched his hand attempting to push it through, but there it stayed, stuck in the slot, forever. It didn't even fall out when the door was opened.

We had savings enough to survive for quite a while. Without working, without doing anything.

A month had passed by the time I got up the steam to go and withdraw from university.

You might surmise that by then it was January, two thousand and five. But you'd be wrong. Judging from the lack of any semblance of shadow on the ground (something I counted on in the absence of a watch) it was still December twelfth, two thousand and four. Ever since that day, the sun hadn't bothered to come out, hadn't bothered to throw so much as a few lousy shadows under things.

I walked through the dazzling limbo of Woodhouse Street, replete with every imaginable neon temptation, and then past the shrunken park with its parterre of syringes pointed at your feet. I came out on Woodhouse Lane, with its bakeries armed with bulging muffins splashed with blueberry blue or banana yellow icing or palaces of sugar or rivers of peach marmalade. And there before me was Hyde Park, immense, a white theater where a sunset was being obscenely enacted, the red head of sun descending, slobbering over the black tops of the trees. But isn't it late in the day for sunset? So, maybe it's not December at all. What month is it?

The answer is automatic, like when you call a toll-free number: "December." You object: "But if the sun is setting at this hour!" And the voice: "December. Thank you for your call."

Then, the street of pubs. Almost every one had an animal in its name, a horse or a chicken. And once you got past the farmyard, there was that other pub, the one they called the Library to make you think you could take a book out. Then the really tall Parkinson Building, the university, an enormous phallic tower with a plaque that says, "The erection of this building is due to Mr. Parkinson." How could it not make you laugh?

At the entrance, the Anglo-Saxon beast-guardians accosted you with a big smile and asked if you'd already heard of the Christian Union.

I went in. In the administrative office, the secretary with the cute nose, the invisible eyelashes, and the freckles must have been, give or take, fourteen years old. I swear that I tried to speak out loud. But the sentence came out in the language of looks.

The girl stared at the complex syntax of my eyes as they first flitted up and then dropped limply into hers.

She said: "Can I help you?"

I enunciated a look.

She said: "Are you ok?"

I emphasized the final syllable by dropping my gaze to my wretched hands.

She said: "I'm sorry but . . . " and she may have been about to call security, or maybe her daddy.

On my hand, I wrote: "I'm withdrawing from university."

She replied on a scrap of paper: "Are you mute?"

"Sort of, but you can speak."

After filling out a variety of forms I returned to the spacious hall of the Parkinson Building. Everywhere, people were walking upright dressed in clothes to cloak the secret devices of dormitory copulation.

My only concern was to stay far from everyone. I checked the notice board for jobs but every announcement said, "Good communication skills and positive team spirit a must," or "Wanted: English native speaker for a survey blah blah." I was about to leave when I noticed a scrap of smaller paper: "Wanted: Italian-English translator." So, being Italian had some use after all, I thought. Ever since the age of seven, when I first moved to that frigid English universe, my nationality had never served any purpose except that of inviting stupid questions about kinds of pasta.

Gagliardi, an Italian washing-machine manufacturer, was looking for someone to translate instruction manuals.

I called the number and forced myself to deflower my silence, though I really had no desire to do so.

It's not that hard: you breathe in and let the words pass from the brain to the vocal cords. It's a vibration, nothing more.

One, two, three! It's ringing.

"Good morning, my name is Camelia Mega, I saw—"

"*Gagliardi Incorporated. If you're interested in the position of translator, visit our offices at Number Six Whitehall Road from 9 a.m. to 12 noon, Monday to Friday. Thank you.*"

I stopped a guy in his tracks. "Excuse me, what's the time?"

"Sorry?"

"What's the time?"

"Sorryyyyyyy?"

"Fuck off!"

I stopped another and asked him the same question. He looked at me, petrified, and ran off. Nobody understood me.

I left the Parkinson Building, and just as I got outside I threw up on a flier advertising the Supercool Student Club.

"Let's meet new people and have fun together!" it said.

I noticed the shape of the "W" from "What's the time?" mixed in with my vomit. Wait, there's the "h"! And if you looked closely at the green lumps you could make out the whole sentence: "What's the time?"

I vomited again, this time it was "Fuck off." The "together" on the flier was covered with a single shot.

When I got to the gray Gagliardi Inc. building I saw a large printed arrow on a sheet of paper taped to a wall of the stairwell that said, "Gagliardi third floor." On the third floor, there were two overweight men without much hair, a fan moving slowly above them, and a calendar of boring still lifes on a peeling wall.

"So what's your name, love?"

"Camelia Mega."

"Ah, you're Italian. Good. Here."

I thumbed through the stack of pages he'd handed me.

For your safety:

During wash cycles the transparent porthole tends to heat up.
Do not force the porthole open for any reason.
Do not allow children near the porthole.

"Ok, when do I have to send it in?"

"What?"

"When do I have to send it in?"

"Sorry, what did you say?"

"When do I have to send it in! Fuck!"

"Ah, sorry, it's just that the way you speak . . . I don't know, it's odd."

I read the text several times on my way home. Actually, I should say as I went down on my home, because, while nobody realizes it, Woodhouse Lane and Headingley form two lurid open thighs that, as they run downhill, converge to form Christopher Road, my street, where all the human race's unsightliness is concentrated in a single macabre focal point.

When I got to my door, a kid with a long nose wanted my mobile phone and money for drugs. I said, "Do not force the porthole open for any reason," and he said, "Bitch."

I watched him walk away enveloped in the pornographic light of sunset, and then went inside, shutting the door on that slaughterhouse of bloodied fleshy clouds.

I vomited a long *Do not force the porthole open for any reason* on the feline roadkill I found yesterday on the street. But what was that feline carcass doing inside?

Oh right, I was planning to use it as a welcome mat.

With my first earnings from the translation job I bought my mother a parrot. We didn't give him a name because, well, neither of us spoke. He was pretty and full of life. Flying about the place, he resuscitated the dull gray of the walls. As I translated she took photos of him with her phone.

The great thing was that I didn't need to talk to translate. The meanings were all there and there was no need for tiring vibrations in the throat. If I wanted to communicate with the two guys from Gagliardi, I used email.

Then, one night, it must have been sometime in December, the doorbell rang. I woke with a start. There on the doorstep was an old woman with dyed blond hair who smelled of new fabric. She was wearing a dark blue suit and her face was as ashen as mine. In her hand was a vase of violets.

I wanted to say, "How can I help you?"

In reply to my silence she whispered that she was my grand-mother, although I had probably forgotten her face. As she spoke, fleshy bread sticks danced around her neck. I moved aside to let her pass and noticed that she had my mother's eyes. That is, my mother had them first, and now this woman did.

She looked at me as she handed me the vase and said, "You resemble your father, that bastard." That single sentence then dissolved into an incomprehensible tsunami of northern Italian dialect that sounded more like French. That was one auditory memory I hadn't retained from my seven years in Turin.

She headed straight for her daughter's room, up the stairs to the second floor, without so much as slowing in front of the two rooms on the floor below, as if she were equipped with radar. Or maybe it was just that my mother stank, and I didn't realize it anymore.

I picked up a pen and wrote on my hand that I had to give my mother a shower tomorrow. I heard my grandmother talking to her daughter.

I took the heartsease into the kitchen. Or maybe they were sweet violets. Certainly, they were not *viole d'amore*. What a great variety of violets there are. All sweet, pretty things. I picked up the scissors and enacted the Spanish Inquisition on their petals.

I went outside to throw away the vase and the mutilated stems.

Before closing the door, I glanced at the street.

You could hear my grandmother's words floating down from my mother's room. It was snowing but it wasn't cold. A kid in a blue hoodie was walking down the street, iPod buds in his ears. He was singing. He didn't care about the snow at all.

My grandmother taught the parrot to talk and my mother taught my grandmother not to talk. In a week my grandmother was perfectly trained. Each morning the two women sat on the sofa with the avian and began a dialogue of silent pauses uninterrupted by words. On the floor above, I worked on my translation.

Opening the porthole and placing clothes inside:

Push the button with the image of the key on it.
The porthole opens.
Caution: the porthole will open only if the machine is properly plugged in.
Before placing the clothes inside, check that there are no animals inside the barrel.

The parrot said, "Leeeeeeeds."

My grandma kept on talking affectionate gazes as her daughter spoke annoyed eyes.

A forbidden season, not winter, moved a restive animal light over the windows. The minute you looked at it, it was gone, swallowed by the darkness. It's hopeless. In Leeds, winter with its freezing breath destroys every other season like the big bad wolf blowing down the houses of the little pigs. And then it buries them beneath snow without even a trace of a funeral.

Every so often my grandma broke the silence by saying "ciao" to the parrot. She wore a tracksuit that was identical to my mother's and one day it was soiled with bird excrement. "Stupid parrot," she said. And he replied, "Ciao."

I spoke a look: *I'll help you get it clean.*

By the third day the feathered beast had learned to say "ciao" in two languages and he couldn't get it out of his head anymore. In fact, the more he said "ciao" the crazier he got, flying here and there knocking into the walls, *ciao ciao ciao ciao hello hello hello.* My mother watched him terrified.

I added *Ni hao*, "hello" in Chinese, to the list just to make him happy.

The parrot replied, "You have to get back to your Chinese studies." Or maybe it was some other kind of avian utterance.

*

When my mother got fed up with her mother I showed the old woman the door. I wanted to say, "I'm really sorry," and, "It's nice to have a grandmother," but she interrupted my thoughts by closing the door behind us and advancing into the cadaveric night of Christopher Road. You could tell from the way she held her crocodile skin handbag that she was angry at having failed in her mission to reanimate my mother. I touched the door handle the way she had touched it, I turned it as if turning door handles was something normal. Now the door was open like a chest wound.

It was snowing.

I could hear the parrot squawking. Maybe my mother was tormenting it because she wanted me back there. Or maybe the poor feathered beast wanted to kill himself. It would be perfectly understandable if he did.

But I continued watching the blue statuette of my grandmother as she walked away and became a freckle in the snow, which happened when she had passed Number Two. It's like boiling point; beyond that limit people become memories.

First, another squawk from the bird, followed by the sound of wings flapping insanely. And outside, nothing. No stars, no vapor trails, nothing. This is what night is on Christopher Road. I mean: this is what it isn't.

So, when you see a cat pass by, you offer it some fish in exchange for a bit of purring. But the cats on Christopher Road only eat human flesh, the flesh of Englishmen, and so you go back inside, back to your winter, back to your crazy mute mother who's got the parrot squeezed between her legs. She's burning his wings with one of my grandmother's still smoldering cigarette butts, and the bird is pecking her legs. It is a battle between nature and culture.

With my mother representing the former.

My open notebook was on the sofa in front of her. The next

sentence to be translated was at the top of the page: "Check that no foreign bodies are placed in the wash."

I extricated the feathered beast and placed him on the floor.

She reclaimed him and put him back where he belonged, saying eyes like, *What do you think you're doing?* Between her legs that variegated body lacking only one color, the color that swallows all others without chewing, Leeds gray twisted and convulsed.

Mamma, stop torturing the parrot it's not his fault that our life stinks!

Livia lifted her wan face. It was Leeds gray, too. Her lips parted, revealing a reliquary full of Leeds-gray teeth tending to yellow. Was she snarling or smiling?

I hurried back to the open door—my grandmother was our only chance. I called her voicelessly. But how could she hear me? Though I could still see her, a tiny speck, she was too far away by then to hear. There were the clouds and the sky and, well, all the things that when you're a child you would never dream of leaving out of your little drawings. I shut the door. Like my mother in Via Vanchiglia putting her pearls and her white gold bracelets back in the safe. As she closed the door, she'd say, "When you're big, my love, these jewels will all be yours."

Then Livia got tired of the parrot. She locked him in the room on the first floor with the queen-sized bed and the crowd of things that go and and and—a Saint Vitus' dance of convulsed movements, a scampering towards death—as they tell the tale of Stefano Mega, at least up to the point where he exits his own story without warning.

I bought her a Polaroid with the money from one of my translations. Beautiful, shiny, and enormous, it was in a shop front not far from my house. I carried it home in the dark: here in Leeds that's how December works, it gets dark before you even realize the sun is up.

As I placed the camera in my mother's long bony hands I noticed the sphinx-shaped stain on the left leg of her tracksuit. We were in the kitchen, which was impregnated with the smell of fried food. I asked her the look, *And that tracksuit Mamma where the fuck did you get it.*

I went back to work. The washing machine company sent me new translation work via email. "During the wash cycle the porthole tends to heat up. Do not force the porthole open for any reason. Be sure to keep children at a safe distance from the porthole."

In the kitchen that evening I found nine identical pictures of the shower drain. The hole took up the entire frame of the photograph, showing a demented tangle of my hair and a thin slaver of foam to the right.

Why are you taking these pictures, Mamma? I thought hard, but she didn't answer.

I closed my translation and went up to her room, but she was asleep, cuddled up with a cushion. She looked dead. Who knows if my father and that woman slept cuddled up like that. But of course they did. They must have done all the things that lovers do, like showering together. I could see the movement of their bodies under the stream of water. I clenched my fists, screwing up the translation. They're fucking under the water. During the wash cycle the porthole tends to heat up.

Sometimes I thought of my grandmother. It was nice to think of something that hadn't died in a ditch. What a shame that despite all her labors the parrot had forgotten how to say "ciao." Maybe he didn't say it anymore because it struck him as a waste, given that nobody replied.

I unlocked the door of the room where my parents used to sleep.

The parrot looked at the window in a strange way, not like a bird but like a woman in a Victorian novel, his eyes lost in a vortex of longing. The sky outside conveyed something to him and to him alone.

Poor parrot, there was nothing else I could do: I threw the cage open and the window, and he flew away without so much as a *ciao*.

There was a lump in my throat: how could I have let him go? "Come back!" I cried, and, oh, it was like drawing your first breath after a game of who can hold their breath the longest. And that's how I started talking again. Again I yelled: "Come back here!" And words, well, they're herd animals, they're never alone, so my "Come back here" brought with it other verbs and complements, like "I'm making pasta" and "It's raining again." These two—"I'm making pasta" and "It's raining again"—turned up two days later on an afternoon that was bleaker than judgment day while my mother was still sleeping and the neighbors' dog was barking like a wretch.

I was on the sofa in the living room futilely searching for a TV channel that showed actual images instead of spastic gray stripes. I was hungry. I was thinking about how my parrot used to watch the bell tower out the window. "I'm making pasta," I yelled loud enough for the words to reach my mother's room, and lo and behold, ten seconds later she was at the top of the stairs, her hair a sebum helmet pushed down over her forehead, dressed in her dragonfly pajamas, with the stain over her breast from the coffee she spilled on herself a month earlier.

She stood there staring me down, like a rancorous princess whom the bad fairy has punished with one hundred years of ugliness.

She said the look, *Go ahead little miss proactive I dare you to say something else.*

"It's raining again," I replied. I felt my gorge rising and I ran to the bathroom but I was too slow. I threw up on my Goofy slippers.

The bilious green pieces looked like an "I" and then a "t," a dribble of apostrophe and then an "s"; another heave and I dumped a lumpy "r" and an "a" and an "i" and "n" and there may even have been an "ing." A disgusting smell of putrefaction. My mother still standing at the top of the stairs. I didn't look at her: I didn't want to hear her eyes saying *Do you see what happens when all of a sudden you start talking again.*

Be quiet!

Don't use that tone of gaze with me!

I ran into my room and gave myself a stern talking to for three hours straight. I spoke about everything, as you do when you run into an old friend you haven't seen for years. I told myself about what it would be like if I hadn't left university and about the beautiful flat where I wanted to live, and about that porcelain geisha I picked up at the Thursday market near the station, and which I'd placed on my bedside table on Victoria Road, and the Englishman who'd sold it to me and the way he smiled at me. He had blue eyes and he was so nice, and as I was walking away I could feel his blue gaze resting on my back. But I spewed it all out, the "g" for geisha and the "n" for nice, the "b" for bedside, and there were greenish dribbles in every corner of the room, dense disgorged letters of the Latin alphabet. I fell asleep doused in its smell and had putrid dreams.

Little by little more words came, and I gagged on them less and less. At first they struck me as so totally useless. I was shocked the world remained unaltered after every utterance. Nor do I find them particularly useful now, but it's not like dogs cease to bark once they realize that their barking doesn't work.

All the same, that day my parrot flew away as I cried, "Come back here." Maybe he flew away because I was telling him not to. I watched him vanish behind the bell tower that rose out of the cemetery.

My mother came running, terrified by my cry, as if right before her eyes a pot, or some other inanimate object that had been beyond suspicion until then, had begun talking. She stared at me with her standard *what's-going-on* look, an all-purpose gaze she reserved for the majority of events that happened around her.

I replied, "Come back."

My grandmother wasn't the last person to come to our house, the dealer was. During my brief trips to the supermarket I often ran into these kids whose plan was to steal my money. Sometimes I gave them a few of the sleeping pills I always carried with me in case of emergency, that is, in case of a sudden desire to end it all, or the need to discover what would become of me if I dropped off in the middle of the street. It's not true that I'm one of those who dwell on death. It's death that dwells on me; it's the window in my mother's room that desperately wants my body to pass through it. I am the erotic dream of windows in former working-class towns. Poor things, there's hardly a single one that actually opens. Try the windows in my house if you don't believe me. Anyway, going back to the kids on Christopher Road, one of them, one day, he must have been thirteen give or take a year, asked me if I wanted some hash. I said yes and invited him home. I was curious. I'd never smoked anything.

"What?" he said

I repeated, "Let's go to my place."

"Sorryyy?"

"My place!"

"Sorryyyyyyyyyyyyy?"

"M-y p-l-a-c-e!!!"

"Whaaaaaaat?"

"Fuck off!"

It was official: my words had been cloistered in my throat too long, and now they no longer worked.

The same thing had happened to my mother by dint of staying shut up in the house for so long. I turned and walked away, and he started following me like a lost dog. I felt nauseous at first, and then seconds later, it happened. I knew it was coming. I ducked behind a shrubbery and vomited.

"What's up, man?"

"No, nothing. I'm anorexic. Leave me alone."

"Whaaat?"

"Yes, you heard right, verbal anorexia. I haven't spoken for ages and now, obviously, every word I speak I vomit . . . My fucking business anyway."

"I don't understand, man."

"Fuck off."

Another load of vomit on the asphalt of Christopher Road, which is well used to it. Its Friday night hobby is greeting rivers of spew that run towards Woodhouse Street like soapsuds, with the heads of kids bent over what's left of their sixteen pints of beer. In fact, Christopher Road is hooked on vomit. It's also the only way to wash away the snow.

I dried my mouth with my hand, the yellowish trails on my fingers looked like an "f" and a "u." One final splatter on the military boots I didn't like anyway. I shook a "c" and a "k" off the metal reinforced toes.

The baby pusher followed me home, walking a few paces behind. It was freezing cold.

We got home and he got the hash ready. While he rolled my mother looked at him askance, and so he said, "Bitch." Around here toddlers learn that word even before they learn to say "Mummy." She didn't reply. It was then that I finally understood that there was nothing more to do. If an insult like that couldn't reactivate her vocal cords then there was really no hope left.

"Bastard," I said to the baby.

"Sorryyyyy?"

"Bastard!"

"Whaaaaat?"

I threw that pimply harbinger of truth out of the house. But then, as he walked away, I watched him from the window, my eyes holding fast to him like a boy to a kite. I even felt my fingers twitch as they searched for the invisible cord.

At Christmas in the year zero I dressed in one of those dresses I'd found in the dumpster. The green one. My bare left arm was cold. But it didn't matter. I spent the whole day at home with my mother, as always.

It wasn't actually Christmas, but it was close enough to turn the flashing lights on and put up a tree, to do all those things other people did. Even on Christopher Road.

We ate in silence. The naked bulb cast a meager intermittent light over us. It wasn't like that before, we had lots of money. No, that's not true; it was like that even before, even when we had had lots of money.

After dinner I suggested a movie on TV, but she shook her head. So, I picked up the bag of garbage and went to throw it out, leaving a stupid movie about Santa Claus on the TV out of spite.

She stopped me at the door and grabbed my arm. She leaned down over the garbage bag and stopped right in the middle, where there was a hole. You could hear the sound of sleigh bells coming from the TV.

The flash popped.

Dragging her feet, she went off to bed.

I left the house. The night was thick, the blackness outside seemed fake, and the houses, each one the same as its neighbor, looked like the set of a low-budget movie. It was like they wanted to be pulled down and moved back to their previous locations, in a real city, where the houses are each different and emit the sounds of living people.

In the dumpster there was a hillock of clothes, freshly cleaned and folded. I took them all and carried them home.

Each piece had some kind of defect. Some had two different sleeves, like the first two I found; the collars were too tight on others. Then there were trousers with the pockets sewn in crooked and T-shirts that didn't hang right.

I arranged all of them carefully in my dresser.

I started going out dressed in the dumpster clothes. That is, I started going out, and I started going out in those clothes. I paraded all that obscene irregularity on the streets, the sleeves on the seats of my pants, the underarm buttons, errors of a sort that no human being could ever have made, and thus divine errors. Indeed, when nuns saw necklines sewn over my butt they invoked Christ and his entire family.

Buttons that ran irregular courses and concluded in some embarrassing cavity or another. Sexy knitwear that came in dolls' sizes. Trousers with three legs.

But I felt perfectly at ease in them. After all, I only went to the supermarket or to behead flowers at the cemetery. Then, one afternoon, I thought what the hell, and I struck out as far as the video store that I used to go to with my father on Sundays. It was in Woodhouse Street, a gray and squalid street filled with takeaways of every imaginable nationality. There was the Chinese takeaway, the Indian, and the Italian; who can say if they'd been arranged alphabetically on purpose. And to the right, the arid park, where a garden of used syringes grew under the swings.

I chose a DVD and went back home. I began renting the same movie every time I went there, *Noi the Albino*, an Icelandic movie where hardly anybody talks and it snows a lot and then one day there's an avalanche and everybody dies. I would go straight home after I'd picked up the movie. But it didn't help: life is like water, and it managed to find its way in through that tiny fissure the world, that brief walk to the video rental store. Wen was standing at a bus stop, as still as a road sign, like the unfortunate man on emergency exit signs, with his legs up in the air, forever frozen in that moment right before making his escape. If I had not been standing on the other side of the street at that precise moment, that little man would have been able to escape my life.

Instead, the number 96 bus stopped and when it drove off again he was still there, looking at me strangely. What the bloody hell did that Chinese boy want? The last thing I needed was someone collecting donations for earthquake relief or some such thing.

The Chinese boy crossed the street. He drew nearer, his footsteps soft. He was slightly taller than me—that is to say, short—but well proportioned. A black shirt made out of appalling acrylic and at least two sizes too big for him fluttered about him like a pirate flag.

Never mind donations for the earthquake in China, I thought. As soon as he opens his mouth I'll tell him that I'm collecting donations for my mother's silence, that I want one pound sterling for every word she hasn't said to me, and that's not all: I want all those words back, too, all in alphabetical order, and he can recite all of them, from A to . . .

He stopped a few centimeters away from me.

It was then that I noticed his very special eyelids free of that unsightly crease that everyone else has. They were smooth and taut, like sheets of paper ready to be written on.

They were white, so white, super white.

Like his narrow nose and delicate ears. Like his round cheeks. Like his small fingers that he extended towards my breasts.

"Eh, what the fuck are you doing?"

"No, no, pardon me, you've got it wrong, it's just . . . Pardon me, can I ask who gave you that dress?"

"Sorry?"

"Who gave you that dress?"

"Yes, I heard you, but I don't understand the question. I bought it in a store naturally."

"Pardon, but really that's not true."

"What do you want from me?"

He looked at me, lost, he looked at the sleeves of my dress that was too tight over my chest, and I looked at his special eyelids.

"Did you get it from the garbage by any chance?"

"That's a ridiculous question."

"Pardon. Are you sure?"

"Of course."

"Pardon, it's just that this dress comes from my shop."

"I'm fed up with this."

He blushed, lowered his eyes, and started chewing his nails.

"Pardon. It's just that we have a terrible tailor. Let me explain . . . you see, he's slightly retarded, mentally, I mean. He makes such a mess of the dresses and I often throw out quite a lot."

"Where is your shop?"

"It's not exactly mine, it's my father's, but he's never there. He lives in Knaresborough."

The noise of a metal shutter. The Pakistani at the video store was opening up.

"*Zai jian.*" I said goodbye in Chinese, though Wen seemed content to stay there raping his own shyness ad nauseam.

"But, you . . . you know Chinese?"

"No, no, very little . . . Three years ago I started studying it at university."

"And then what happened?"

"Then everyone fell into a ditch."

"What do you mean? Everyone who?"

"My father, my mother, me, and the Chinese characters, too. Ha ha."

"Pardon, but I don't understand what you mean."

The crack of broken fingernails.

"I was only joking. Bye."

When I got home my mother was sitting on the floor in the living room. She waved me over and handed me three of her most recent photographs.

A harsh light shone over her face and went fallow in the obtuse folds of her wrinkles, rotting in her brown eyes. They used to be sea blue, her eyes. Then the sea fell into a ditch and filled with mud. Her hair, which she no longer washed, had turned from blond to brown. Who knows, maybe staying at home all day every day, far from the light, has had something to do with it as well. Her entire body was the wrong color, even her gray tracksuit—it had faded in the washing machine and turned the color of a rat.

The photos were of a hole that had recently formed in the blue curtains in her room.

"I'll buy more curtains this week at the market," I said, caressing her hair.

She said the look called *Have you really got it in you to walk that far?* And I replied with the one called *Don't worry, I'll take care of everything.*

Yes, I know you pity me, but what good does that do me? Copy all that compassion of yours and paste it into *your* story.

I carried the laptop down to the kitchen, put some water on to boil, and inserted the DVD. To my horror I discovered that, while the cover was right, the movie I had rented was not the Icelandic one at all. I'd been suckered into renting some fucking American comedy where everybody is smiling and there's even a soundtrack.

On my way to take the DVD back I stopped and looked at the bus stop and thought about the Chinese boy. He'd thrown the clothes away on my street, so his shop must be somewhere in the neighborhood. Why, then, had I never seen it?

I turned into Headingley Lane.

You could feel the incandescent vegetation and the dark brown Victorian homes behind those walls, and the voices of people, and the ethereal laughter coming from far-off like in a dream or during the opening credits of a horror movie, as they prepare you for the splatter that will put an end to some halcyon scene or another.

Anyway, it's the same old trick with the scarecrows. The reality behind those walls is different: rooftops impaled on long poles and illuminated by fluorescent lights, polished plastic plants, and crude transistor radios that imitate the voices of people in love with life. It's all a fake, an act meant to convince me that there's a part of Leeds, the best part, that Italian girls orphaned of their fathers cannot see.

I passed a newsstand and a florist, where I bought a red rose that I deflowered with my Swiss Army pocketknife and then left in pieces in the gutter, a sadistic smile of petals around a grate. I pushed them all into the sewer. Me, insensitive? Oh, please.

Further ahead, on a billboard across from the supermarket there was a famous model stretched out on the grass in a bikini. She wore headphones over her ears; there was an enormous daisy to the side of her perky-nosed, high-cheekboned face, and a very yellow sun hanging in the sky above her. It must have been summer on the billboard. To the inhabitants of Leeds a billboard showing summer is like one advertising *Star Wars*.

The woman was saying that her batteries lasted forever. Those were her last words, because two men in dark-colored tank tops were plastering, strip after strip, and another image over her. The daisy became a headlight. The D-cup breasts became a license plate. Her delectable nose, cold gray metal. Even those feline eyes, metal. Her long fingers, a wheel.

The woman on the grass became a Lancia Delta driven by Richard Gere. That's all you saw, at least at Twenty-Three

Headingley Lane, but if you turned on the TV at home you could see Richard Gere driving all the way to Tibet to bequeath his sacred handprint in the snow to a group of Buddhist monks.

I walked further and then there it was, on the corner, a shop marked by two Chinese paper lanterns and four splashes of red paint indicating a name I couldn't read.

Beneath, the transcription: *Shouxue shangdian.*

There were little bells hanging from a gigantic red wooden cat. The bells jingled as I entered and I jumped. It was a small, tidy shop. The boy I'd seen at the bus stop was sitting behind the register, his torso bent over the counter, his fingernails in his mouth, his lank hair falling over his downcast eyes. His entire body was engaged in a monstrous effort to become invisible. He struck me as one of those people who are afraid of life. God, as if it were final or something!

"Ah, *ni hao*! So, you know my shop."

I said a look of salutation.

The walls were mandarin colored. I squinted, my eyes irritated. A row of knitted sweaters, beginning with a sand-colored poncho, ran from the register to the door, and parallel to that there was a row of skirts and trousers that terminated at a white plastic curtain behind which was a dressing room. To the left of the dressing room, half hidden by the last few skirts, was a red door.

Above the door was a faded decal of a big smiling woman whose hair was tied in two buns on the sides of her head. She was holding a long parchment filled with Chinese writing.

"How much do these jeans cost?"

"Ten pounds."

"Can I try them on?"

"Yes, certainly, the dressing room is over there." He lowered his eyes.

I pulled the curtain closed and changed into the jeans. Through the crack between the curtain and the doorjamb I could see the big smiling woman. What the hell was written on that parchment? I tried to remember something, anything, of what I had learned, but each ideogram I brought to mind took me to task for my blockheadedness.

I looked at myself in the mirror. The jeans, with their indecent blue sequins, offended my thighs. I slipped straight back into my gray dress with the crooked buttons.

"How were they?"

"Bad."

"Too big?"

"No, do you have something more . . . "

"More?"

"I don't know."

"Try these on, the ones with flowers, they're cute. Should I get you a size 4?"

"I'm going home."

A genocide of fingernails and then he lifted his eyes, his round face reddening like a moon becoming the sun.

"Wait."

"What is it?"

"Are you still interested in studying Chinese?"

I smiled at him. In my mother tongue, that smile meant *I don't think so*; in my mother's tongue you say the same thing with an oblique glance.

"Because, you know, I give private lessons to university students."

"I'm not a university student anymore."

"Yes, pardon, I know, but . . . "

"Ciao."

He said, "Ciao," and I left to the jingling of the little bells. From outside I looked at him and he looked at me, his white face framed in the window, his eyes like black but harmless fingernails.

I turned for home. It was already dark. The truth is, in Leeds it's actually impossible to head home while it's still light, it does-n't matter at what time you head off.

The takeaways gave me a neon salute as I passed, and I slalomed through bags of garbage scattered along the entire length of Christopher Road. I read somewhere that astronauts are trained in Iceland because the landscape is similar to what they'll encounter on the moon. If that's true then they must bring terminally ill patients to Leeds to get them used to death.

My mother was sleeping on the sofa with the Polaroid cam-era around her neck. I shook her shoulder. It was like touching the trunk of a dry tree. Four pictures of holes in the Swiss cheese fell to the floor. One, a close-up, looked like a woman's thigh.

She looked *what's up?* at me. I replied with a new look that didn't exist in our language. It meant *Let's-buy-a-dog, do-you-want-a-hot-chocolate, let's-go-to-London-like-we-used-to-and-take-in-a-fashion-show-at-Southwark.*

But she couldn't understand any of it.

I went to my room feeling discouraged. The sheets of paper from Gagliardi Inc. were scattered on the floor and the table and on my pillow. On the chair, the defective clothes I'd col-lected looked like the hides of skinned animals.

I picked up the one with two different sleeves and in a rush of sadistic creativity cut one of the sleeves off with a pair of scis-sors. Then I halved the skirt and sewed the part I'd cut off onto another dress, diagonally, like a seatbelt. I carried on in that fashion for hours, taking untold pleasure in slashing trousers, mutilating pockets, mixing up buttons, and grafting ugly collars onto even uglier dresses. Until the ugliness was dazzling, flaw-less, until the clothes I'd found in the dumpster were no longer enough, I had to transplant fabric from the clothes in my wardrobe. The dumpster clothes became even uglier, especially when I started to make hybrids, of the kind that are dreamed up in laboratories, mixing the teddy bears off my pajamas with the fringes on my evening gowns, god the excitement of it.

*

The following day, when I went down to throw the garbage out, I found the jeans I'd tried on at the shop in the dumpster. I fished them out and took them home. I cut out all the sequins as if they were malignant tumors, and replaced them with zigzag miscarriages from my pajamas. Then I punished the pockets with some canvas patches cut from my backpack. I continued, wounding every pair of pants I owned with patches of red canvas, more or less where blood would run down your leg if you were an Italian journalist who was fucking an English woman and you died in a ditch.

I pulled on the jeans and left for the Chinese shop. The sky had turned dark, though it wasn't evening yet. But that's Leeds-style desynchronosis for you. And being out of sync had become chronic in Leeds—you just had to look around to see the effects of it. And a bonus of scattered snowstorms and high winds.

"Why did you throw them out?"

"*Ni hao!* Throw out what?"

"These jeans."

"Pardon, but I've never seen those jeans before."

"What are you talking about, they're yours. I just altered them a bit."

"Oh, those. Well, after you left I realized that the stitching was crooked."

"No, it wasn't."

"So why didn't you buy them?"

"How come you throw things in a dumpster so far from your shop?"

"It's a long story. If I tell you, you'll think that we're idiots."

"We? You and who? No, don't worry, I don't want to hear any stories. I'm leaving. Ciao."

"Wait, listen, have you changed your mind about the Chinese lessons by any chance?"

And that's when I solved the enigma of the little man on the exit sign. It's not that he can't escape, it's that he really doesn't want to. He's one of those who remain.

"What are you talking about? Stop it! I'm through with university."

"But why?"

"I told you."

"No, you . . . You said something about a ditch, but I didn't really understand . . . Your university fell into a ditch?"

"Ha. No, the University of Leeds is still in one piece."

"So, what is the problem?"

"My father died. After that, I didn't feel like studying anymore. Are you happy now?"

"I'm sorry. My ex-girlfriend died, too."

"You think that makes me feel better?"

"Pardon."

"Don't worry. I'm going now, *zai jian.*"

"No. Can we just try? Please. I'm sure you're good at it. Or do you have something to do?"

"When?"

"Now."

"It's not that I have something to do, but—"

"Sit down here, I'll go and get the book."

"What, now?"

"Why not, c'mon!"

I replied *I'm not sure* in the language of looks. He smiled at me ever so slightly. But during my mute period, I had abolished smiles together with all the other communicative grimaces of human beings.

He disappeared into a room.

And returned with an old red textbook in hand.

He picked up a spiral bound notebook with a cover showing two yellow flowers.

He drew four lines on the first pages. The tones.

Sure, I remember. There's the high even one, the one that falls a bit and then rises, the one that falls further and rises less, and then the one that just falls. That last one's me. In fact, it makes the sound of him crashing into the ditch.

"Now let's see if you remember how to pronounce them. I'm going to write down a word."

"All right."

He wrote a word out and gave it to me. Now it was mine forever. It was an "E." An "E" is a good start, less authoritarian than an "A" and not as definitive as a "U." I was pretty happy with my "E." In Chinese there can never be an "E" alone; there is no such thing as that carefree sing-along we call the alphabet. An "E" must mean something, "blackmail," or "moth," or perhaps "evil."

Mine was "to provide for" because it had a horizontal dash above it.

"Go on, read."

I flung out the sound shamelessly.

"Yes, but you mustn't let your voice fall."

"I can't stay up there."

"Sure you can, try again."

"EEEE."

"No, your voice has to be steady, even."

"That's what I'm doing"

"No, you go down."

I wanted to scream I was so angry. I focused on the E, on its upright bearing, like a chainsaw, and on the horizontal dash, the first tone, above it. The last time I saw that straight line indicating the high-pitched, steady sound was at the hospital. My father's face was scored with dried blood. His eyes still saw me, but then the monitor whined and the zigzag line went flat. It was the first tone. The monitor made a sound like the first tone. With my pen I scribbled all over the yellow heads of the flowers on the cover.

"Do it again!"

"EEE."

"Very good."

Shortly after that the lesson and I left.

Outside there was a sky.

A sun.

I carried on repeating "E" to myself.

For me, an Italian, that "E" didn't mean "to provide for" at all. It meant "e," that is, "and," a conjunction. How, then, could it fail to conjoin me to somebody?

The next day was Tuesday. I remember the day distinctly because it was then that December suddenly began to specify itself in days of the week.

This must have alarmed the local authorities. I mean, I once read that if one day is followed by another, and then another, sooner or later December might actually end and January begin, and then after a while, March, and at that rate the next thing you know it would be summer. I suspect, however, that this is only a publicity stunt on the part of Burberry, who are trying to sell their new £300 sundress.

The onset of specificity happened right after the lesson. There was a light drizzle, a pretend rain. I was on foot chasing a slow sunset that spread over the entire street like ketchup.

When I had gotten to the shop the Chinese boy told me to call him Wen and he started to doodle in a notebook. He was wearing an oversized black sweater, a pair of faded jeans, and bright red Converse knockoffs on his feet. He sat behind the cash register, and I sat on the other side of the counter. An army of invisible people spied on us from deep within the hanging garments.

He handed me the notebook. In the middle of the page he'd made a mysterious lopsided T.

A lambda.

A decapitated crucifix.

"What is it?"

"It's the key, or radical, for 'person.' Each ideogram containing that key has something to do with people. This, on the other hand, is the key for 'animal.' You see how it looks like a tail?"

"How many keys are there?"

The more questions I asked the redder he became. The redder he became the more questions I asked. He didn't move his feet. They remained within a square formed by a floor tile.

"Lots. Many ideograms are formed in that way, adding a key to an existing one."

"But, then, if all you have to do is add these keys . . . The number of possible Chinese characters is infinite."

"I wouldn't know. In a way, yes."

He sat down again and opened a book of exercises.

"In reality, Chinese characters were grouped into their keys only in the year one hundred and twenty, so that people could look them up in dictionaries. It's an arbitrary grouping."

"And before that how did you look them up in dictionaries?"

He looked at me, punching a hole in my face with his exceedingly black eyes. He always had a hovering look on his face, like a hound that has been left on the highway and found his way home.

"Before that, you couldn't look them up."

"Are you serious?"

"I think so."

He opened the huge dictionary to page three. It was divided into five columns that were in turn divided into even smaller numbered columns.

"I'll teach you how to look things up in the dictionary. Let's say you're looking for the ideogram I've written here."

"It's cute."

"What?"

"This ideogram."

"You see that its key is 'person,' right? It's composed of two strokes, so go to number two."

He indicated the second column with his small finger.

"Ah. And I can find the ideogram there?"

"No. You can find a list of keys formed of two strokes. Look for the one that means 'person,' and that will send you to another number, see, in this case nineteen."

"It's really complicated."

"No, it's easy! Just go to nineteen!"

"And there I'll find the meaning of the ideogram?"

"No, there you'll find more numbered columns. You have to count the remaining strokes in the character, that is, the total number of strokes minus those of the key, and go to the corresponding column."

"My brain is going up in smoke."

"No, no, it's done, you just have to go to the column . . . "

"And there, finally, it will tell me what the ideogram means."

"No, there you'll find a list of ideograms with the same number of strokes, you choose yours, and it tells you how to pronounce it."

"Not the meaning?"

"No, first you have to know how to pronounce it, and then you can look for the meaning in the alphabetical part of the dictionary. See, this here means 'benevolence.'"

"I'm amazed, I don't remember it being so difficult to find characters."

He smiled, pleased with himself, and softly closed the dictionary. My head was spinning. That looking for words could be an adventure was a thrilling prospect. I thought of my translations for the corporation as daring missions. Like a gold prospector, I was panning for meaning.

Who knows how things would be different if you had to

search for every word in English in the same way, if all the English words were hermetically sealed. And to peek into the meaning of just one you had to enact that crazy ritual of strokes and numbers, columns and pages and keys from start to finish.

"See you Thursday, Camelia?"

"Yes, but what day is it today?"

"Pardon, what do you mean what day is it? Tuesday, right?"

I pulled on my old purple leather coat, the one with two holes like eyes at the front.

"And how many are there?" I asked him.

"What?"

"What do you mean what? Keys!"

"Well, it depends on the dictionary . . . "

"Fine, ciao."

Wen kept on smiling.

Perhaps the keys do not only open the room of Bluebeard's dead wives.

On the way home I bought a wall calendar with sports cars on it. It was on display at the newsstand and had surely been there for ages because it had turned a yellow color and the corners were curled. It was ugly and I hate cars and anyone in them, but it was a calendar. Then I stopped by the market and I bought some fabric. The stout lady with the light blue eyes put it in a shiny red bag for me and said, "Thanks, love." You never get used to it, the fact that in Leeds complete strangers call you "love," but sometimes you need it.

Inside it was night, although it couldn't have been later than four o'clock. My mother was waiting for me in front of the TV. I hung the calendar up on the wall directly above her head and she eyed it with the look you reserve for someone who shows up uninvited. Then she turned back to *Will & Grace*.

I told her the look *Please react let's go see Woody Allen's lat-*

est movie or I could take you to the Russian circus on Woodhouse Lane do you like tightrope walkers?

She replied with the look, *Still banging on about this going out business.* I went to my room and I looked at the shiny red packet. I finally drew the fabric out. There was a bit of black velvet, some gray cotton with green arabesques, some polka-dot canvas, and blue Chinese silk with big flowers on it that looked like peonies.

I deflowered the velvet, turning it into two round patches that I stitched tight onto the pink dress at nipple level. Then I cut the fabric with all those arabesques on it into long strips and began to inflict gray and green grates onto the frayed breasts of the wool sweaters.

When night fell I picked up the overalls and administered a dose of red polka-dot measles, scattered here and there between the bust darts and the crotch of the trousers. Then, in a flush of idiosyncrasy, I stuck a large peony right between the legs. I laughed, laughed at all the unslakable cunts of all the English lovers of Italian journalists.

Sometimes a rare species of spring comes to Leeds and everyone treats it with religious respect; they take their shoes off in Hyde Park, like Muslims in their mosques; they dress in cream colored linen as if donning sacred tunics, as if the wearers of that holy raiment were participating in some ceremony.

But naturally spring here is nothing but one of those scarecrows that Leeds loves to parade. Only the English believe it's spring, because for them there's nothing out of the ordinary about March gardenias marooned under the snow. They believe that England is the undisputed champion of the whole world.

I don't call it spring. I call it Leeds. Just Leeds. My mother doesn't call it anything at all because she doesn't talk.

She used to be a flautist and she played at weddings in Turin. It was at a March wedding, as she translated the spring into high soft notes, standing in front of a Mozart score, dressed in turquoise, which she adored, tall in her azure heels, radiant with the vivid sky of her eyes, that she met him.

My father stood up from his table and approached her, offering his congratulations. She often told me the story. That day she said thank you in her typically faint voice.

He was the groom's cousin. He was dressed in tails, and her whole face lifted into a smile. She took her flute apart, and, with a perfume-ad smile, she said goodbye to the violinist, the cellist, the violist.

So what if I wasn't there? I know perfectly well how my mother acted. Her heels touching the floor with nary a sound as she folded her music stand and put her sheet music away.

Him saying, "Do you have an umbrella?"

Her: "No, actually I don't."

"I'll accompany you to your car."

"That's very kind of you. Are you a musician, too?"

"Ha, no. I tried the piano when I was a boy but it was a disaster. No, I'm an editor at *La gente*, it's an independent newspaper distributed by—"

"Maybe I've read your work, who knows, may I ask your name?"

Say whoremonger. Say betrayer. Say swine.

Or Stefano Mega, a name with a vague Nintendo echo. And my mother was already making her way through the confused crowd, leaving with him from the villa on the edge of town.

Walking slowly to her white Nissan Micra.

Taking small steps on the tiny points of her stilettos.

Her upright carriage. You never heard her breathe cough sneeze.

She immaterialized the world.

"Here's my number, take it, Miss...." And he gave her his yellow business card, which read "Editor, *La gente*." That business card is in a drawer in the locked room now that everything is inside out, like a pullover with the stitching on the outside.

She said, "No, first names please. My name is Livia."

Despite the umbrella, she caught a cold that day, and while she was at home gulping down aspirin, he called her. They made arrangements to meet that Saturday at the Museum of the Moving Image because he was a cinema buff.

"You know, Livia, you're fantastic."

"What are you talking about, I am not."

"Have you ever been in the room where you lie down on sofas while they project erotic movies on the ceiling?"

"Where, at the museum? No, I've never been to the museum, I know I should really have gone, but you know when things are in your own backyard—"

"Yes, I know. In fact, I'd never heard you play before that wedding. You're so . . . "

"I've never read you either."

"That's because *La gente* is a crappy newspaper."

"I'm sure you write well."

"No, not really, but I like it, all I do is write. I go to bed with my computer, hah."

After the telephone call she went to play, but no sound came from the flute.

"Why not?" I asked her when I was five and lying in my wood frame bed in Via Vanchiglia as she took my temperature.

"Because when you hurt, your flute hurts too, sweetheart."

"No it doesn't, don't tell fibs."

"It does, it's true. When you've got a temperature you don't have much breath, so you can't play."

Then, at that point in the story, gigantic fridges and toilet-shaped chairs enter the picture, but not because the story has turned into a bedtime fairytale, rather because it was there that my parents kissed, the following Saturday, beneath the gigantic fridge in the Museum of the Moving Image, between an orange the size of a football and a carton of milk as big as a streetlight, and behind them, where the screams came from, there were the

WC-chairs, on which you could view *The Exorcist* and *Poltergeist.*

"Shit, you know you're really pretty?"

His large fingers on her cover-girl waist.

"No, Stefano, what are you talking about, I'm not that pretty."

"Yes, you are, you're a real bombshell, you know what I'd like to do to you now?"

My mother smiling among the gigantic fruit with that crazy blue sidelong glance of hers, the golden cascade of her hair splashing onto her cheeks.

"And if you count to three, my love . . . Only three short years later . . . "

"One, two, three . . . But I already know what happens."

"You do? You already know?" she said, tickling me. On the other side of the window the halos of the streetlights on via Vanchiglia. The light struck a corner of the polka-dot curtains, through the window came the sound of people on the street below, and I turned back to look at her. She was smiling at me.

"Yes, of course I know, you got married. Why do you always tell me the same story?"

Because there's a trick. If you start at their wedding day and count to three you jump to year minus three and then to the year zero—my mother in the kitchen with her greasy mouse-colored hair eating macaroni bolognaise with her hands. My mother lifts her eyes, belches, her elbows on the table, her hands as limp as fish fins. Her fingers, her long musician's fingers, limp like the fingers of the dead, suspended above the table, soiled with meat, her knuckles prominent like large rings that he never gave her.

She grabs her Polaroid.

I say, "You know I've started studying Chinese again?"

She points the lens at two holes in my leather coat.

I say, "You know today's Wednesday?"

She shoots.

The lessons with Wen were good. It was good to walk to the shop. When I left the house it was light outside, when I came home it was dark.

Key to light: "fire."

Key to darkness: "darkness"

I discovered that some ideograms were their own keys. Others are made of so many different pieces that you never know which is the key. I also discovered that even without trying air flows through my lungs, in and out, ad infinitum.

On the way home I devoured a kebab without onion and I picked up a movie, as if going out because the sun has come out from behind the clouds, moving about because the sun, too, rises and sets, and does so without even once falling into a ditch, as if all this was the most natural thing in the world. As if it were natural to let air fall into one's lungs. And above my lungs there were crooked patches and oddly matched buttons, overstated slits or collars in the shape of claws.

"Say it with me: *Xianzai ji dian?*"

"*Xianzai ji dian.* What does it mean?"

"It means, 'What time is it?' Now, answer."

"*Xianzai si dian.* Right?"

"No."

"No?"

"I mean, the sentence is right, but it's six o'clock, not four."

"Yeah, ok. What's it matter?"

"What do you mean, what's it matter? Sorry, there is something: you come every day at a different time. Could we, perhaps, pardon, I don't know, decide a time, please?"

"Why?"

"Can we decide a time?"

"I'd have to buy a watch."

"Don't you even have one at home?"

"I had one, but it's in the apartment on Victoria Road."

"Listen, let's see each other again on the thirteenth at six, ok?"

On the thirteenth at six. It sounded like a combination on the Battleship game board.

"The thirteenth of what?"

"Of what? Of December, of course."

"Of course. Yes, ok. I'm going now, Wen."

He leaned forward awkwardly with his hand slightly raised. That's how he says ciao. I exchanged his salutation in a more aggressive fashion, according to tradition, my fingers and arm fully extended. I was already out the door.

Outside, in the dead center of a shriveled flowerbed, a poppy was waiting for me. I should probably say that it was magnificent. It was tremendously red, beyond any concept of red. Its stem sliced the air perfectly, tall, greener than green; its petals opened to the sun like thighs, they flowed sensuously out from the swollen corolla that was smothered in bee kisses.

What right did it have to be so beautiful? Who gave nature the right to conspire so constantly against ugliness, to extend its creeping embrace over the houses of men, to exhume a poppy like that from the dry throat of an English winter? I ground its corpse under my boots.

When I was small I was convinced that flowers grew everywhere. When you couldn't see them it was because they were buried like shells under the sand and you just had to dig them up. What a dope. You don't have to search for beauty; the minute you let your guard down nature slaps you in the face with beauty. If you're not careful, as you're walking into the center of town you find yourself in the midst of an orgy of yellow flowers, and what choice do you have at that point but to destroy them? I murdered them one by one, I choked them inside my bag with a necromancer's pride.

"You're going to die anyway," I said to the terminal petunia that was expiring against my leg. "There's a hole with your name on it, where dogs piss and people fuck, and everything dies, people and dogs, all together, even if they've tried to close the hole with concrete, and you fool, do you think your beauty is going to save you?"

I turned around to see Wen's white face looking at me. I put the flower down. The corolla was decimated, there wasn't a single petal left. But it was still yellow, yellow like the sun.

I was exhausted when got to my street. It was still snowing. And to think that the mayor's campaign slogan was "less winter for everybody."

I shook my umbrella, looked around in search of life forms. Nothing. I ordered the crew to set a course for earth, and opened the dumpster as if it were my spaceship.

Inside there was a yellow tunic that was unlikely to fit over anybody's head. When did he throw it in there? Maybe the tailor throws things in there himself sometimes. I thought back to "Let's see each other on the thirteenth at six." It was one of those sentences that belonged to other people and couldn't enter my house.

In fact, as I entered the house and passed my mother she amputated the sentence from my brain with a single glance.

In fact, "thirteenth" and "at six" crumbled into loose letters.

In fact, the calendar with the sports cars on it was under the sofa open to a page showing a Ferrari defaced by dust and barbecue sauce, the names of the days and the months hidden beneath mounds of moldy English imitation Parmesan cheese.

I ran into my room. I operated on the neckline of the tunic at once—an utterly successful operation that even included an ugly red ribbon removed from a slipper and sewed into the crotch, like a chastity belt.

I put the Icelandic movie into the computer and lay down on the sofa. It wasn't the Icelandic movie. It was a fucking French comedy. Two French people talking in French and laughing in French. I fell asleep to the tedious drone of their "r"s.

*

"What do you mean, you're sorry? I want my money back. It's the second time!"

"I'm sorry."

"I have more sorrys than I can stand, you're not sorry at all! And how old are you anyway, fourteen? And they put you here at the cash register so you can make a mess of the DVDs, so you can put them in the wrong cases. And what else do you do with the discs? I bet you eat your meals at the counter, scattering crumbs all over them, don't you? You know nothing about the cinema, shame on you! Now what are you doing, crying?"

"I'm sorry . . . "

I couldn't understand anything anymore. The Pakistani boy was in tears. While he wasn't looking I pulled my Chinese workbook out of my backpack and tore out a page. I slipped the ideogram for "to be born" between *Death in Venice* and *Death Proof.*

At home I wrote ideograms with better pens, newer ones that were still shiny and vibrant.

In no time at all Chinese words had infested all of my notebooks: an ideographic regime. I forgot them as easily as I learned them, but the ones I forgot always came back, I recognized them in shadows on the ceiling, I found them in the swirls of dust under my bed. But that time in front of the weeping video store boy, that was the first time I'd ever let my ideograms out into the world, and on the way home I mentally practiced writing "to be born," the word I'd left like a seed in the store. But it was gone already, completely forgotten.

I found the scotch tape at home and angrily stuck two nouns written in black ink onto the kitchen wall. Wen had told me many times that it was a good way not to forget them.

My mother lifted her head out of the shortbread and with her mouth covered in crumbs she stared at the characters like they were strangers.

"You say, '*fan*,' Mamma. It means 'food.' And the other one means 'trip.'"

She replied with the look called *What do you think you're doing.*

I defied her, unsheathing another ideogram and sticking it up on the steel sideboard. It was an enormous and complicated "to speak in a nasally voice," the Chinese character with the most strokes of any, a whopping thirty-nine.

She stood up. *Just look at you Camelia you go from verbal anorexia to some kind of bulimia.*

"You don't understand anything, Mamma."

She turned red and clenched her bony fists, countering with a sharp look named *You're making a mistake.*

In only five days our house was filled with presences, in every corner, Chinese characters on white paper. They fluttered in the breeze like ghosts. But we were the dead; they were the living.

Vibrant spontaneous brushstrokes, each one named according to size and direction. And if you happened to know the secret of the keys you could understand what those words were doing in the world, in your house, on your fridge. You could understand what my mother and I were doing there.

On December twelfth, I bought a clock. It was round and shiny with a pink plastic frame. On the walk home I held it in my arms, as if it were a baby. It was snowing. When I got to Christopher Road it was like reaching the last page in a novel, the page that's all white and you're still thinking about the ending, but not the ending, no, the ending isn't thinking of you at all, all that's left of him is a white page, dull white, it's-over-now-so-piss-off white.

At home, my mother was asleep with her mouth open and her head on the table. I hung the clock on the wall beside the fridge, between "trip" and "red," because they were the most joyful ideograms in the kitchen. It went tick tock, just as you'd expect from a clock.

I moved it into my room, in order to sleep better.

Christmas came. Then it went back to where it had come from. Wen told me that Chinese people don't celebrate it anyway. He even opened the shop on Tuesday the twenty-fifth.

Tuesday, December twenty-fifth. It has a ring to it. Arranging time by the days of the week and month and even numbering them was a new drug for me, and it went to my head.

On Friday January fourth, two thousand and eight, I discovered the following words on the palm of my hand: "Give Mamma a shower." So, the day after, I decided that the day after I would decide to shove my mother under the shower faucet the following day.

At first, she resisted, but then I closed the shower box by force. Her pounding died down after a while and I handed her the sponge. With another sponge I began rubbing her chest, which was slack and dry like the skin on a turtle's legs. Over time, her skin had grown flaccid like an old dress and her breasts drooped lifelessly.

"Mamma, you should take better care of yourself. Do you hear me?"

I rubbed the dirty brown brick of foam over her neck, brushed her broken hair, and got the dirt out from under her fingernails.

"Check that no foreign bodies are placed in the wash."

I dried her. We went to her room and I gave her her tracksuit, which I had washed and ironed and left for two nights in a drawer full of lavender sacs. Then, my head throbbing, I went downstairs, shut myself in my room, and threw open the Chinese dictionary.

There the keys were neatly arranged in columns, there were grass and mountains, sun and the sky, bamboo and gold. It contained the whole world. And the following day, like every Tuesday, I would go to learn it.

On weekends I sat down at my desk early in the morning. From the window I could see houses, each one the same as mine, and people coming into the street to throw their garbage out and then going back in. I could see the foil-colored sky, a gray that light could not penetrate, a gray beyond day or night, good and evil.

There were these kids who came out of nowhere to steal from an old woman. They would ask if they could use her mobile phone and when she handed it over, smiling, they ran off. Behind them an African came out to throw away the garbage.

Key to "garbage," the same as that to "inspire."

I picked up the black writing pen, my favorite, with its soft nib like a brush, and copied out the ideograms, devoting an entire page to each, at times even more. I wrote them over and over again until I had mastered them, until I could write them without looking. Page after page. A vast meadow sowed thousands of years ago with incontrovertible meanings that nobody can now change.

I ate with my mother, went to throw the garbage out, collected the day's disfigured garments and went back to writing. It wasn't true that I was the fourth tone. If I just kept copying I could be the one that falls and then rises. I was rising.

Sunday, January thirteenth, at ten past ten in the morning I left my Chinese at home and I went to the flea market and bought three notebooks with blue paper. On the way home I rented the Icelandic movie. I was looking at the cover as I left the store, which is why I didn't notice the daisy coming my way. I wasn't going towards it, no. A daisy, a vegetal Lolita dressed in a wedding gown by Gucci, was waiting for me in the grass, waiting there like death. She was there to make me live, yet somehow she ended up under my shoe, seven little muddy ribbons of white, the green stem sticking out from under my shoe like the leg of an earthquake victim.

When I peeled it off the bottom of my shoe, night fell.

I had turned to ice by the time I got home.

I put the DVD in the computer.

My mother came into the living room looking angry.

I thought it was because I hadn't left her enough cereal, but instead she gestured for me to follow her into her room. Frowning, she pointed to the ideogram for "hate" on the wall and the translation into English that I'd scribbled on the table. But I hadn't meant it seriously, it wasn't indelible ink. Well, maybe I was just a little serious. "Mamma, why should you be angry? You don't give a shit about this house anymore."

Yes, but you don't hate me do you.

"Of course not, don't look at me like that, what do you want me to write, 'love'? Sorry, but the key to love resembles a claw, you see, right above the heart. And look, look at 'hate,' over the heart there's night, and nobody gets hurt."

I went into the kitchen and opened the fridge.

From the computer came the demented theme song of an English TV series.

I put the dead daisy in the Heineken bottle.

January progressed without any regrets at no longer being December.

My Chinese improved. Winter did not. No, not even when the sun slurped up the snow and belched one thunderous storm after another over us, not even then. But what did I care. I was in the shop with Wen.

Thursday, January seventeenth, at 6:11 he said, "Chinese is a morphosyllabic language. Every syllable," he explained, "is a word unto itself."

He wrote out a long sentence.

"See? You can divide the words into syllables but every syllable still has a meaning."

Like wasps. You can pull them apart but they'll scurry about all the same. I imagined the ideograms at home pulling themselves off the wall and taking flight and I saw my mother mutilating them with the scissors, and the little pieces of paper still twitching on the floor.

The red cat jingled in the wind, the windowpanes rattled, Wen was already putting his parka on and looking through the windows at the interminable kingdom of snow outside. "Look," he said.

"What is it?"

"The city. It looks dead. There's nothing out there."

"But the snow's going to stop tomorrow, Wen. The forecast says it will."

"I'm not so sure."

"Neither am I. I always feel like the weather guy is having us on."

He smiled with his head down, he bit his nails, his gaze hidden inside nothingness.

"I'm afraid I can't do it, Wen."

"Do what?"

"Learn Chinese. All those characters . . . I don't know. There are too many."

"Come to my place."

"What?"

"Pardon, I mean . . . I'd like to invite you to my home."

"Where do you live?"

"In a sweet little town with a castle."

"Ah, and I suppose there's even a dragon guarding it?"

"What, sorry?"

"No, I'm joking, don't make that face."

"What dragon?"

"It was a joke. A dragon, like in fairytales, a dragon guarding the castle, breathing fire on anyone who comes near . . . "

"Dragons spout water from their mouths, not fire."

"Stop it."

"Pardon, but it's the truth. In China dragons spout water."

"Really, is that what you say?"

"Oh, and they also carry souls up to the heavens. Here, in Europe, do they carry souls to heaven?"

"Mm . . . I don't know. Let's hope so."

"Maybe here it's the pope who carries souls to heaven?"

"Ha! What are you talking about?"

"Pardon, it's that I heard that you people believe the pope talks to God. I've always thought how strange that is. But, listen, does God reply when the pope talks to him?"

His face was all red and he was looking down at his feet.

"Wen, let's forget about Catholics, I don't understand them either."

"They're mysterious. Strange. I don't understand these things."

"They do even stranger things. Just think that when they're in church they eat Christ's body and drink His blood."

"I don't believe it."

"Don't think about it, Wen. Listen, when should I come to your house?"

"Whenever you want. We can study Chinese. And I'll cook *jiaozi* for you."

"Huh?"

"Chinese ravioli. You'll like them. We can roll them together if you want. Can you come on Sunday? The town is called Knaresborough."

"Sure. At what time?"

He raised his fist.

"What are you doing? Are you going to hit me?"

"Huh? No, at ten, I mean. Don't you know how to count with your hands?"

"We indicate ten with all ten fingers up, Wen."

He laughed. He took the keys out of the cash register, and we left. It had stopped snowing, and there was a tiny sun low in the sky like a footnote. The note would have said: "Based on a life suddenly full of possibilities."

I was a few meters behind Wen, my eyes fixed on the red of his parka. The traces of snow on the asphalt were of a complicated white, furrowed, a bit like frayed cotton, the cotton of old forgotten cushions in the attic. But then someone comes along and puts them back where they belong, on a sofa full of people, in a city where it's no longer December, and the sun is even out and there's a marvelous Chinese boy in a red parka.

Once upon a time my mother played every Sunday on Pearl Radio and while she was playing my dad took me places. Around his neck he wore a leather bound notebook he'd bought in Liverpool on which were written the words, "The Beatles Story." But it had nothing to do with a story, it's the name of a museum. Every now and again he'd stop and sit down on a bench to write something. He was looking for his scoop, he said, but I think he was taking notes for a novel.

He would look at me and smile. I was still a child. He'd say, "You know, little one, stories are everywhere." And the thought terrified me. When I got home I'd close the door of my room and hide under the covers.

On the morning of Sunday, January twentieth, at nine-fifteen and seven seconds I boarded the train for Knaresborough.

Key to "train": "fire."

The car started moving and at some point, after stopping at a station on the outskirts of town where two flabby English people in flip-flops were reading gossip magazines, I found myself suddenly out of Leeds.

I hadn't dared hope for so much.

Through the window, sheep, horses, and cows appeared in

quick succession. And farmhouses, each one different from the last. And more cows, more horses. They wouldn't stop coming, like pop-up windows when you're navigating online. And beneath them, a single stretch of brilliant green that hurt your eyes to look at. I couldn't believe it.

The entire city of Leeds, with its Victorian buildings and its noisy nightclubs, its McDonald's and its shopping malls, and above all with the poor dreariness of my neighborhood, was held hostage by an enormous and thrillingly inhuman universe. Leeds was a purulent freckle on an immense and dazzling body that I was ashamed of not having discovered before.

I put my fingers and my nose against the glass and I would have left them there forever.

More sheep. Outside. Two red-and-white poles for horse jumping left now to their own devices. Beech trees with enormous trunks and crowns that looked at if they'd just left the hairdresser.

Each one of those mighty trees and every blade of grass and every white horse and spectacular flower, all of that beauty arranged strategically on the other side of the glass, like cakes in a bakery seen by some poor starving urchin, all of it there to tell me, "Go home, Wen could never like you."

I got off at a tiny, desolate station. Alongside the tracks, in front of the closed bar, there was a row of tall striking flowers, the kind that you'd need an executioner to cut. Stems like lamp-posts, petals like the tongues of lions, corollas like the romantic streetlights on roads that are not Christopher Road.

I opened the gate and, as Wen had instructed me, began walking down towards the antique shop. I passed by checker-board houses with knights painted on the closed windows. Wen was there, standing in front of the little white shop with round windows and a wooden door, and the name in black italic lettering that read, "Antiques."

He greeted me by moving his hand ever so slightly, as if her were undecided about the right gesture to make. I returned his greeting energetically, lifting my entire arm. And then I was standing in front of him.

He was looking down. I inspected his pullover—a Levi's knockoff with an extra "e." He wore old leather moccasins on his feet.

We went down the street to the river. It was still and black.

On the other side of the river there were a few white or sand-colored houses, and on the riverbank lots of bare, dry trees, one next to the other, an alphabet of twisted branches tracing strange formulas in the air. I was just about to decipher it when Wen raised his eyes from the tangle of weeds and dead plants and thornbushes that covered the banks of the river like a witch's hair, and said, "How do you say, 'This place is beautiful?'"

Me: "*Zhege difang hen piaoliang.*"

Him: "I like this place."

Me: "*Wo xihuan zhege difang.*"

Him: "I like you a lot."

Me: "*Wo hen xihuan ni.*"

"No, don't translate, I mean I like you, Camelia, you're so pretty."

He was incredibly red in the face.

"I like you too, Wen. *Who ye xihuan ni.*"

He took my hand in his small, limp, and sweaty hand, and said, "Now tell me how you say, 'We're alone in this place'?"

"*Zai zhege difang zhi zai women.*"

"No, no, no. You say *Zhege difang zhi you women.*"

"What? But that means, 'This place only has us.'"

"Yes, but that's how you say it."

"It's weird. It makes me sad."

"That sentence? Why?"

"Because, if you say it like that, I don't know . . . it's like this place suffers from loneliness because in the world it only has us."

We walked for a while. There was no one around, just us and our chameleon words going from English to Chinese without withering.

We protected them inside our united hands. We protected them from the cold and the wind and from things that die.

"Camelia, now translate, 'It's a nice day today.'"

"Why are the sentences I have to translate so sappy?"

"What?"

"Nothing. *Jintian tianqi hen hao.*"

"Good! Now . . . 'I'm reading a nice book.'"

Silence while I thought about the translation for "book." But even the silence would need to be translated. There was no escape.

"*Wo zai kan yi ben hen youyisi de xiaoshou.*"

"Right. Now . . . "

"Do you like teaching, Wen?"

"I love it. I mean, I really love it."

"I don't get it. Don't you feel a huge, an enormous responsibility?"

"Why? No, it's great and that's all."

He smiled down at the ground, at the weeds, he never looked at me.

"And what are your other students like? Better than me, right?"

"No, you're much better. The others have a lot of difficulties; I have to explain things to them many times. I've never had a student like you, you learn fast, and it's clear you're enthusiastic about it."

"Yes, you're right. I am enthusiastic . . . Never, anyone? Really?"

The sound of fingernails splitting.

"Hm . . . there was another one, two years ago, that loved learning languages like you, and you know what, she was pretty like you too?"

"I'm not prett—"

"I've only got two students now, anyway. They're in Knaresborough like me, which makes it easy, they come to my place when they're not working."

"Hm."

"What are you thinking about?"

"My mother. I'm a little worried."

"Sorry, but why?"

"I don't know. I don't know if she's eaten the soup I made for her. Or if she needs me for anything."

"Why don't you call her?"

"She doesn't answer the phone."

"Why not?"

"It's complicated."

"Meaning?"

"She's not . . . normal. I mean . . . Don't worry about it, you wouldn't understand."

"Maybe I would. I have a brother who's not normal."

"What do you mean?"

"You're wearing his clothes right now."

"No, your brother is the tailor you were telling me about?"

"Exactly."

"How old is he?"

"Twenty-five, two years older than me. And you?"

I told him I was twenty-one after almost a minute, as if it were the result of some complicated equation.

We got to the castle as the sun was setting behind the tower. From the top of the stairs there was an incredible view of the town. In its midst was a bridge suspended over the water like the splendid, arched body of Christ, a body that knows everything and feels everything and for those very reasons wants to die.

I froze.

That was my father's dead body. And my mother's moribund body.

Wen caressed me again with Chinese words but I could no longer understand them, I took them in the face as they came, consonants, vowels, and tones, without masticating them with my brain.

Suddenly, they all had the fourth tone, the one where the voice goes down, down into a ditch.

Wen took me by the shoulders.

"So, what is it that you don't understand, Camelia?"

"Everything."

"In Chinese, I mean."

"The keys."

"I explained it to you, don't you remember? You need them to look up characters in the dictionary."

"Yes, I know, but when a character contains more than one key, how do you know which is the right one, the one that leads you to the ideogram you're looking for?"

"There is no surefire way, you try them all."

"Let's try this: you tell me a word and I'll tell you the right key."

He released my hand.

"Why? That doesn't make any sense, Camelia, I don't understand."

"Didn't you tell me that if you understand the keys of the ideograms you can guess what kind of word it is?"

"Yes, but what's the point? It's an exercise that makes no sense."

"It does for me. Are you my teacher or not? I want to learn."

He turned red. He nodded, his eyes downcast.

He points at the river.

I sketch two drops and a diagonal waterfall.

He points at the sun.

I sketch a rectangle sliced down the middle.

He points at the ground.

I sketch a cross with a horizontal plinth.

He points at the bridge.

"I don't know the key to bridge."

"No, I wanted to say that it's very pretty, isn't it?"

It hadn't occurred to me. I hadn't asked whether or not it was pretty. Death had leaped to my eyes before the bridge itself. It was the bridge's most evident characteristic, more than the shape or the color.

I had to look at it again. Wen's question was like that movie game where they show you an action scene and instead of asking you who died, they ask what color were the murderer's shoes.

The bridge. The bridge was two stone "M"s written in block letters.

Mortification and Martyrdom.

It met itself in the water, and beneath the river's surface its thick stone hooves became the soft legs of a woman. The houses beyond it were painted checkerboard, others were the color of sand. All different heights, scattered like happy little tin boxes from Harrogate, a town famous for chocolate, with jellybeans and toffee in the windows.

Wen looked at the sheet of paper in my hand.

"You're good."

"No, I'm not. You're too kind."

"No, I mean it. You're smart. You're an exemplary woman, like the women in *Lienü zhuan*!"

"Write it down here."

"What?"

"'Exemplary women,' in Chinese."

"Okay."

He turned red. He held the pen lightly in his fingers. He wrote, "*lie nü*."

"But Wen, in the word 'exemplary,' isn't the key to the right 'knife'?"

"Yes."

"And the one to the left, isn't it the same as in 'death'?"

"Yes, of course."

"Tell me some more ideograms that have death in them."

"That have only that key or that have the entire ideogram?"

"There are characters that have the entire ideogram for death in them?"

"Well, there was 'dirty' that used to have death inside it, but not anymore."

"What do you mean not anymore?"

"You know that Chinese characters were simplified in the fifties, don't you? They removed some parts . . . Sorry, I have to make a telephone call?"

He walked away slowly, went down the stairs, and disappeared leaving me alone with the bridge. Two blue ducks flew across the water and the river's surface rippled and thickened like the skin that forms on milk when you warm it too much.

I shut my eyes. To sleep forever, on standby, to book a one-way ticket to the place where Stefano Mega's rotten soul lies, wherever that may be. To sleep while the ducks move over the surface, making out that movement is an easy thing.

I took out the container of sleeping pills and emptied it in the palm of my hand. I put them in my mouth, all of them, a Eucharist. This is the body of my father, who died to free us from our sins.

It's easy to free oneself from sin, easier than it is to free a fish from its bones. All you have to do is close the front door, like my mother and I did on the day of the accident. To shut out the world's lunatic spinning wheels with a simple turn of the door handle.

Stories, gone.

Movies, gone.

Everything, gone.

You, gone. Wait, Daddy, I'm coming.

The pills tasted like a blackcurrant milkshake.

One Sunday, when I was small, I remember, December happened. Suddenly. Or, at the very least, it was December enough to provoke one's hatred for everything in the universe. But with my yellow glove inside my father's black one, I was walking along Hyde Park and watching the snow-laden trees pass before me; it was like looking through a shop window at a row of wedding gowns, like he and I were getting married in secret.

On those long and snowy Sunday walks he would take my hand as we left the video rental shop. In his other hand he carried *Kwaidan* or another of the classic Japanese movies he loved, and I would ask him, "What's this one about, Papa?"

"It's a collection of many stories, honey, the best one tells the story of a blind monk who plays the *biwa* really well, and so all the ghosts come looking for him to hear him play."

"Isn't he afraid?"

"No, because he knows they're ghosts. He's blind, you see? But then the other monks discover his secret and you know what they do to chase away the ghosts forever?"

"I give up."

"They cover his entire body with Chinese characters. But they forget to paint his ear, so the ghosts come and pull it off."

"It's scary. I don't want to hear any more stories, Papa."

"But honey, that's impossible: stories are everywhere. You just have to look at the people on the street, or turn on the TV, or—"

"Stop it! I don't want any more stories!"

I'd removed my hand from his now. I ran to the trees and began pulling off buds and leaves. I didn't spare a single one. My gloves were thick with resin and dirt.

My father, in his light brown bomber jacket, yelled: "Camelia, come back here. What do you think you're doing?"

Other people, so many, walking around everywhere.

It was happening more and more often. Every Sunday, after a whole week, including Saturday, during which he worked late and she played the flute at home with me, my father and I became the happy heroes of Leeds. We would go all the way to the market, walking between old buildings and kebab vendors, past stores selling shoes that were imitations of other shoes. We'd lose ourselves in the market full of ugly household linen and old CDs and colored flower vases that light up.

Or we'd get a blackcurrant milkshake at Fruity-Joe, on the top floor. He would stand in front of me, and with a straw in my mouth I would dangle my legs as I drank.

I watched people pass through the half-moon window, their lives seemed small from up there and they weren't so scary.

Then we'd be off again, even happier than before, my hands in the shell of his. We'd pick her up and then go home, together. And then and then and then. Sunday was always full of and thens.

My father stood in front of Sainsbury's and scribbled something in his leatherbound notebook, and then he swept up my hand in his again and we were on the move. He told me for the hundredth time, "Honey, stories are everywhere," and ruined everything. All of a sudden, a crowd of people capable of thinking acting injuring and killing materialized around the single body that was my father and I, our hands joined. Everything was ruined. No longer were we alone and safe and immortal.

I asked him to play rock-paper-scissors, but he said, "No more playing, Camelia, Mamma is waiting for us at the radio station."

She was waiting for us inside her own story.

And inside the stories of her fellow musicians, and those of the show's producers, and her parents and her childhood and her feelings for all the people she knew and those she would know, a story for each person, stories past and stories yet to come, isn't it crazy? To become ubiquitous, collective, collectible, isn't it crazy?

Wasn't it enough for her to be the incontestable heroine of my story and my father's story? No, it wasn't enough. I was the only one who felt that one story was enough. As far as everyone else was concerned, having only one story was like being a Cyclops.

We went along Harewood Street and every time I pointed he said, "No, not yet."

We got to the radio station, and her unparalleled lips kissed so many cheeks before they drew themselves level with mine. Look, there they are, her other stories have a face and a nose and hands and thoughts. Then I would stretch both arms out and we'd walk, all three, holding hands. But their greeting had been cold, as if their *ciao*s were foreign words, and they walked alone, and I too was alone. She was radiant and untouchable like utopia, her flute pressed over her heart; he, tormented, a writer. Then there was me.

"And who was that guy with the moustache, he's new?"

"Don't shout, Stefano. He's the producer of the Italian program I was telling you about."

"You like him, don't you? He's your type, of course he is, like that other one, what was his name, the one who played the oboe."

"Oh, stop it. Please."

"What, you haven't told me if he was good at playing yet, right? Did he play you well?"

"I said stop shouting. She's starting to cry. And, for heaven's sake, stop bringing it up over and over. I've had enough."

"You see, Livia? You've made your daughter cry."

Then he died and his story ended. Livia and Camelia Mega deserve special thanks for their precious collaboration during the writing. And you see the alphabetical index, from the A for "Afternoons we go to fuck in Grosvenor Road" to the T for

"Turpey, Liz"? Then the cover art with my mother's face streaked with tears.

One understands why storytellers were banished from China in the sixties.

Wen emerged from behind the stone stairs and came towards me, his eyes lowered. I could see his very special eyelids, his body. I watched his gaze lift in search of mine.

I spat the pills out onto a spray of narcissus.

Wen opened his mouth and said, "What was that you threw away?" I opened my mouth and kissed him. A long kiss. I closed my eyes, opened them, closed them again. And opened them again. I looked around at that place that had only us.

February began and its beginning was contagious. Everything developed a habit of ceaselessly starting.

For example, I started to enjoy wandering around town. The shops full of things, the desire to buy everything, to wear a different sweater to each lesson. And the sun started to rise promptly every three hours to remind me that I had a reason to live. And on my TV's one station, the shows were always starting without waiting for the end. It was a bedlam of opening credits—no sooner had the opening credits of one show ended than others began.

Something even started in my body, in my brain, on my skin. What mysterious movements of blood and warmth, what dreams!

I often found myself near the window, where there was a weird, you might even say warm, breeze. I watched the dirty snow melting and the grass pushing up from below and I thought of Wen. But without averting my gaze, for if I had looked away for even a second, the snow would have slunk back to where it had been, like on those magic sand writing slates.

Of course, it's not like I had a lot to think about. Except for obvious thoughts, that is, thoughts that didn't really need me to think them. But of all those thoughts, only the ones concerning Wen didn't fall into the ditch.

My mother appeared in the room, her thin lips smeared with toothpaste. I waved her over to a seat. "Look at that sunset!" She answered me with a reproachful look that is translated *The sun doesn't interest me*, and she left.

On Friday, February eighth, at two twenty-two and twenty-two seconds in the afternoon, the TV news heralded a day of great winds. That afternoon began the wild flight of the objects.

The first thing to move was my mother's music stand. The wind gave it a slap and sent it hurtling headlong down the stairs. I found it on the floor, crippled, its rectangular head twisted behind its body. I thought it was crying but it was only the sound of the wind.

And that was only the beginning. For two whole days my notebooks slid off shelves, and my clothes fell off chairs. To say nothing of the ferine fugue of my ideograms. The wind ripped them from the walls and whisked them off to the most arcane places in the house. I found a preposition of place down between the cushion and the armrest on the couch, and a "to send" inside the letter chute; a twelve-stroke bird spotted an open window and shot through it never to be seen again.

"Mamma," I said, "why did you open the window? Go and close it." But she just turned slowly and looked at me. She was the only thing there that didn't seem to want to move. So I closed the window, but the wind pushed back, and it flew open again, the glass shook and fussed, and in the end I was struck by the desire to do something too. I jumped around to an aerobics lesson on Channel 4 and danced to music videos by pop singers I detested.

I sat and watched movies and wrote keys on my hand, every single one I saw: a hairy tail for dog, ice for cold, a tree for bed, silk for the red of her coat, a mouth for the question she asks him, three mouths for his insulting reply, and if I was not careful, the mouths multiplied, becoming six, because there can never be an end to it.

I could play that game all night, snapping things into that univocal logic. I could get the better of sleep.

"Mamma, why aren't you dressed? I left your pajamas on the bed."

It was night. It was Saturday, February sixteenth, at nine o'clock. It was the world. It was our brick house in the midst of other brick houses. From the street, you could hear the voices of people out and about either enjoying themselves or waiting to mug a little old lady. Or both.

My mother was sitting on the checkered bedspread, her back slightly curved, the skin of her stomach slack, and her eyelids swollen. The theme song of yet another TV series was playing in the living room. Awkwardly, she picked up the cotton pajama top with the dragonflies on it, and pointed at the light; she wanted me to turn it off. But instead with the red marker I was still holding, I wrote the key for "fire" on her back.

You make it with four diagonal lines that look like meteorites depicted in the glorious instant that they are about to puncture the Earth.

Slumped there with one sleeve on and the other not, Livia was already asleep. I went downstairs to watch the Icelandic movie.

The wind had shoved the DVD under the couch, and it took me a good half hour to find it. The case contained an American movie about four kids who lock themselves underground in a hole to avoid going on a field trip. They give the key to another kid who stays outside, but then that kid doesn't come back to let them out and everyone dies except the main character. I fell asleep before the end and had dreams that were not nightmares.

I awoke at 10:11 in the morning. The sun had staked a claim to the entire living room, including the couch, the bicycles, and the ceiling. From outside came the sounds of living things: people, cars, dogs, light rain. That very reddish red of the magic marker was still on my fingers.

All of a sudden spring arrived in Wen's shop. I mean, the springtime of clothes arrived. An orgy of yellows and light blues and whites, pale pinks and bold reds. Cotton skirts, belted smocks, capri pants, three-quarter length T-shirts, flower-print blouses. Sequins, bright plastic buttons, veils, embroidered or transparent cotton, frilly needleworked pieces, puffy sleeves, the kinds of things hobbits would wear. And a few days later spring itself arrived, I mean the one outside, not the springtime of fashion. And it arrived early, considering it was only February

Apparently, even Leeds springs, like the winters, are terribly presumptuous. They think they can make all the flowers bloom, even the ones that are wilted. Off they go spreading sunshine on the dry petals, saying, "Arise and walk," in the language of birds. It chirps and shines brightly until it has resuscitated every petal, every corolla, every gerbera corpse, until every just-born bud has been uncocooned. Woodhouse Street is full of botanical Lazaruses.

One-hundred-year-old lilies, corpulent roses, carnations with alien petals that reached the ground. Rows and rows of chlorophyll miracles, pollen vortexes. When the bees saw those God-given riches they went mad and stung themselves to death like samurai.

Of course it could never be satisfied, the Leeds spring. That spring wanted to go down in history. It wanted time to begin ticking with it. It wanted to make even inanimate things blossom, things like clothes and cars.

Wen's shop front was a triumph of shimmering yellow light, like rivers of sequins on a dress destined for anything but mutilation.

A dress that I will love forever if now he slips it off me with his small, white fingers.

"Are you listening, Camelia? What are you thinking about? You have to keep your wrist steady, and move your arms."

"I know, but it's not comfortable."

"At first it's not. And, anyway, you're the one who insists on writing with a brush. You know that we write everyday things with a pen, don't you?"

I moved my arm as best I could but it was wrapped in the heavy wool of that gray dress with the high neck and the plastic shopping bag sewn over the belly. Yes, I know I haven't mentioned it before, but you can hardly expect me to mail a catalog to your house, can you?

Wen continued correcting me; he held my brush using his thumb and forefinger, as if it were a fragile insect. Every one of his gestures was minute and full of care for the world.

"You see, like this, Camelia."

"That's how I was doing it."

"No, each character has to stay inside an ideal square."

"Sorry, a what square?"

"An ideal square. Imaginary, understand?"

"Right."

Chinese people take writing very seriously. Wen told me that a long time ago calligraphers were buried with their brushes and inkwells.

My brush had a special wood handle made from a tree that only grows in China and that smells of tea. Buddhists make their prayer beads out of the same wood. It was Wen's. It belonged to his divorced father, who lived in Knaresborough. That fantastic brush came from the market in Liulichang, Beijing, near their old neighborhood. Apparently there are all kinds of handles: white porcelain ones with blue dragons on them, ones made with marqueted wood, or even jade.

"You wrote it wrong again."

"What?"

"This one, the character for 'force.' Look, the first stroke has to curl backwards, like this."

He held down the paper with his fingers and elongated the first stroke of my "force" by a millimeter. I took the brush back and copied it. Then I moved on to the character "desire," but he grabbed my hand, "No, you see, you're making another mistake."

"Why?"

"Because this part here, the part sloping down, has to look like a human arm."

"What are you talking about, Wen?"

"Don't look at me like that, it's written in an important manual of calligraphy!"

"But what does it mean?"

"I'll explain it better on Tuesday. It's seven o'clock already."

He stood up. I got up, too, knocking a shirt onto the floor.

He came nearer and leaned down to pick it up. The red cat jingled twice.

I grabbed his wrist.

"What is it, Camelia?" he said. "I'm sorry if I was mean."

I wrote that desire from before on the palm of his hand. You pronounce it, *xi*. Seven strokes, a cross at the top, like an interdiction. The key is "piece of fabric."

Without looking at me, Wen said, "Yes, that's right, that's how you write it."

I rolled up his sleeve. "Sit down for a minute, Wen." He sat back down behind the cash register and looked at me strangely. He was wearing a yellow plaid shirt and shapeless jeans.

I sat down as well, in front of him. I took hold of his arm again and stretched it across the table over a hillock of receipts.

I wrote the word "desire" on his wrist again, and wrote it again a little further up, and I continued, continued to desire him feverishly for the whole length of his arm.

I desired my way up over his veins and into the crook of his elbow, on that skin as insanely white as the waxed faces of the Peking Opera.

I slowed my pen where the strokes had to be thicker and stopped it in time where they were supposed to be narrow. Wen's mobile phone emitted the sound of a Chinese pop song.

"Don't answer, wait, look, if that stroke is supposed to be a human arm, what should the little stroke at the top of 'happy' be?"

"Um . . . an eye."

I came around behind the counter, next to him, so close that the air he exhaled became all mine. His mobile stopped ringing and Wen started to breathe harder.

"Close your eyes a second, Wen."

"What? Why, sorry?"

"Don't be so worried, I'm only doing my exercises, close your eyes!"

He obeyed. I traced "happiness," which is pronounced *gaoxing*, on his eyelid. First tone plus fourth tone. Sixteen strokes in all.

"Sorry, Camelia, but—"

"What is it? You're all red, for what reason?"

"No, Camelia, it's just that, sorry, I have to—"

"Relax."

I spread "happiness" over his round cheeks and along his nose, some fell onto his shirt. I took it off so that it wouldn't dirty his shirt even more.

He looked at me, red as anything. "Sorry, but that's enough now, ok?"

"What are you talking about, sit still for a second, don't worry."

Sweat sliced the "happiness" on his temple in half. So, I wrote another larger one on his shoulder, and then one on the other shoulder, and all around them I declined it until it became a "contentedness" consisting of eighteen strokes and then a "serenity" of nineteen with the key "green" to the left and the key "war" to the right. I continued until I had filled his shoulders. "Life," I wrote on his shining hairless chest. Fourteen strokes, the first ideogram is the one for "to be born," the second is the one that, if you add "street," it becomes "exit." And "city," and "person" and again "life," because you can never have enough. His back was straight and his fists clenched. "I have to do the shopping, Camelia."

"Wait a minute. Don't get up."

I wrote "satisfaction" around his navel, and a little higher up, "enjoyment," and around them I wrote every other ideogram I knew: the ones for "cat" and "lion," "tears, "mountain," "malice," and "to talk with a nasally voice," "fog" and "grin," and I went lower, my fingers reached the buttons of his trousers.

"No, that's enough, Camelia, I have to go, it's late, I'm sorry." The chair made a racket as he pushed it across the floor. I dropped my pen.

"But, what . . . are you leaving me here like this?"

He was on his feet wiping his face with a handkerchief.

"I'm sorry."

"What do you mean sorry? Fuck, Wen, I thought you . . . I though we . . . "

"No, no, you're right, I like you a lot, Camelia, really."

"Then, why?"

I stood up, walked closer to him and put my lips close to his cheek, which had become a black mess. He jerked his head away. "It's better if we just stay friends."

"Like an idiot, I thought I meant something to you."

"Of course you mean something to me."

"What?"

"Sorry, what?"

"What do I mean?"

In front of me, as I tried to breathe, he wiped the handkerchief carefully over his stomach. He murdered the ideograms that I had made, ideograms that mean nothing yet they are signifying wholes, morphosyllabic, or however it is you say it. I grabbed hold of Wen's shoulders and started rubbing up and down and he said, "Please, leave me alone."

Morphosyllabic slaughter. The clean, careful strokes became obscene marks. "Happiness" looked like a cat that had been run over, "serenity" a pigeon with broken wings, "contentedness" as well, and ink was oozing from its crushed head but I felt no fucking pity.

My head was on fire. I was shaking like a lunatic, "You piece of shit, throw that fucking handkerchief away."

"Ok, I'll throw it away, but don't be so angry, I like you, but—"

"Fuck, tell me why!"

He released himself from my grip and started to close his shirt, forever. One button after another, two seconds each. Slow but nervous movements. His mobile started ringing again. Wen answered and began talking in Chinese. I couldn't understand a thing. I was sweating. I caught a glimpse of the sky, which, through the lying storefront window, reached me swollen with blue like one of those pool mattresses you use in the summer.

The telephone call continued. Do not force the porthole open for any reason. You'd be better off killing it, strangling it with nylon scarves, until it begs forgiveness.

Wen hung up. I was ashamed. I was ashamed of all the things I'd done in my life and all the words I'd said, and my mother's face stared at me severely from under the denim skirts to the right of the cash register where Wen was sorting through some lightweight cream-colored shirts. The plastic eyes holding those shirts closed were my mother's, and over and over again they said, *I told you so.*

Hers were the invisible arms inside the sleeves, hers the neck that swelled the nylon scarves hanging next to the window; no, it wasn't the wind, it was her. Everything was her, except my reflection in the shop window, my pitch-black-hair-big-nose reflection. Wen took a filthy Bugs Bunny keychain from the drawer and put it in his pocket, saying, "Sorry, I have to go." My reflection like a faded decal on the glass, and on the wall across the street, and on the roofs of the fabulous houses beyond the wall. And on the bluer than blue sky. My reflection spat in the face of the world's beauty.

He put his mobile phone in his pocket. "I have to close the shop."

The shame of not having been loyal to my mother right to the end. Of having betrayed our silence, having gone naked before a world that was no longer ours.

He handed me my mulch-green backpack with the streaks of mud and ketchup and the keychain hooked on it of which only a steel ring remained.

"You're a shit, Wen, I'm never coming back to your shop."

I raised my eyes and only then noticed a boy standing completely still in front of the dressing room.

"Who the fuck are you?"

Wen spun around, surprised. The boy didn't reply. He was tall, his eyes were big, startled, and his mouth slanted downwards. He was wearing a yellow sweater emblazoned with the words, "Juicy fun in the sun."

"Get back in there, Jimmy."

He didn't move for a couple of seconds and then went back behind the red door.

"Who was that?"

"My brother."

"How long had he been standing there?"

"I don't know."

I left.

It was freezing outside and it was dark. But the neon lights lit up every corner of Headingley Lane to show everyone my tear-and-snot-stained face, my red puffy eyes, my messy hair, my hands stained with that damned ink, and my body humiliated and even more virgin than before.

Somebody shoves me and I stumble. It's a girl in baby blue dressed as a fairy. She walks by me, sees me, and laughs, her boyfriend in the Superman cape holds her around the waist and says sweet English nothings to her that only she understands. Behind them, there's a naked boy wearing a diaper and sucking on a pacifier who walks hand in hand with Sailor Moon, who smiles, her blond pigtails swaying all the way down to her feet, and when they see me they start to laugh. I turn, hold my breath, I breathe in through my nose until it burns.

The newsstand is still open. There's a calendar depicting baby cats bundled together in a basket, and in front of that, a blond Papa Smurf with his blue-painted skin is kissing Lisa Simpson, who's pressed against a pole, laughing and panting, her back bent, saying, "I love you." She won't stop saying it, not even when the smiling Arab closes the newsstand and answers his mobile phone using long Arab words that are clearly words of love. "I love you," says Lisa Simpson over and over like a fire alarm bursting my eardrum until she has burst my soul. It doesn't stop when I run, because couples pour out of the One Stop Shop, each one with an overflowing grocery bag in their hands.

The man in the green shirt laughs and as she's kissing him she drops the bag, ten thousand perfectly round pink peaches tumble out, and raspberries, too, and the tub of coconut ice cream, and there, next to her on the footpath the boy in shorts takes a sip from a bottle of Japanese prune liquor that he's just opened and passes it to his girlfriend with the braids. She replies in Danish, in Swedish, who knows, but I'm certain she says, "I love you," and my whole body aches.

It starts to rain. At first it's light, then hard. Rain, replete with its odor of things lived, the air becoming a poison gas of things past now returning, the dawn of living memories.

My legs are moving still. Like the tail of a garden lizard when the lizard is dead.

From behind the wall of forbidden beauty come lowered tones, remixed ten thousand times, layers upon layers. Beyoncé and Scissor Sisters, and the techno song of Tori Amos, an orgy of beats and broken voices, Whitney Houston crying out that she will love you forever, then disappearing behind the laughter of people; it must be a party, one of those parties you can only go to as a couple.

Two Power Rangers in acrylic armor cut in front of me, one has his iridescent hands on Heidi's hips, the other takes the hand of a short-skirted Minnie. The Power Rangers go into Lawson's to buy cider. Minnie turns, sees me, and laughs at me behind her papier-mâché mask. Heidi in her red-and-yellow dress laughs too, and they exchange secret words in English, a Morse code of consonants and vowels.

The rain gets heavier. I continue running. My muscles burn and I feel sick to my stomach. I avoid the transvestite lovers, but they're everywhere, they march two-by-two to the pubs of Woodhouse lane, the Happy Chick, the White Horse, and the Library, where the only use they have for books is to lean on them as they pen love letters. And they all laugh at me, repeating over and over again, "I love you," without even stopping to draw breath, including George Bush, who is feeling up Fred Flintstone, and Grandma Duck, with her tongue on the check of Freddy Krueger. They don't stop for a second, they continue to walk, anxious to fill their mouths with high alcohol content beers and the tongues of their partners, for no other reason than to demonstrate to me that there's a whole lotta love in the world, but none of it for me.

It's called the Otley Run, this game, this pub crawl in drag that lasts all night, until its participants are illuminated or at least in bed with the boys they adore. It's called life, this game that all humans play but me. They're called houses, those places on Woodhouse Street bursting with contented boyfriends and girlfriends eating peanuts and cheesecake who, when they see me, start laughing. It's called candlelight, the glow coming from the neon signs, Nino's pizza joint and Tom's fish & chips for only three pounds, that light up the windows of these houses as if it were daytime. Tonight these lovers will party until they drop, just so they can display themselves before me, laugh at me, so they can break my heart into little pieces and sew it onto their old clothes, the clothes they give to their cleaning lady, who then throws them into the garbage. They are called parties and laughter and all-nighters. They are called marriages. Children. Grandchildren. Photos and memories and souvenirs brought home from trips. Sweet little words magnetized on the fridge. Affectionate phrases in the obits.

I am almost to Christopher Road but what does it matter anyway. Two women kiss languidly next to the Chinese restaurant, the redhead recites a love poem in Bulgarian, or Russian, and the other woman replies in an English full of "u"s so I won't understand. A boy caresses a brunette's hair inside the fish & chip shop. My Adidas are waterlogged, and the bag I sewed onto my dress is full of water. I bite my lip until I can taste the warm blood. On the 96 bus, which is passing slowly, and on the yellow bicycle that races past and misses me by a hair's breadth, and in the crowded taxi that splashes mud on me up to my knees, there is nothing but people holding tight to other people and laughing at me.

And on the street, under the rain, people snuggle close and walk, they wear clothes that have been given to them as gifts wrapped in shiny paper bodies that have been warmed against other bodies.

All this, all this effort of love, when they could just as easily have sent me one of those priests who used to knock on doors once upon a time to tell me: "Remember you must die."

When I got home, dripping wet and covered in mud, I emptied my wardrobe and threw all my clothes on the table, both the clothes I'd found in the dumpster and the old ones bought in stores. I got the scissors. I cut everything into pieces. I cut furiously until I could cut no more, until my clothes were a pile of ash.

My mother appeared. She was drinking from a carton of milk, the Polaroid camera around her neck. Her fingernails were dirty, the inner corners of her eyes were marked with green pebbles. The carton made a noise as she sucked the air from it. She threw it on the floor and licked her lips.

"Mamma, fuck, go back to your room."

Don't cry Camelia.

"I'm not crying. I don't cry. I told you to leave."

Instead, she lifted the heavy body of the Polaroid above her head and pointed it at a hole in the ceiling.

But . . . ? Since when had that hole been there?

It was as big as an apple and through it you could see the ceiling of the room above mine. That is, my mother's room.

You could even see a damp stain on her ceiling.

She closed one eye and looked through the viewfinder.

And if you count to three, my love . . .

But I already know what happened.

One.

Stefano Mega has sex with Liz Turpey in the Chrysler.

Two.

Wen doesn't want to have sex with me.

Three.

I let myself die in the hole where my father died.

Flash.

The photo poked out of the camera. She pulled it out. From

the hole in my ceiling, out of focus, the distant stain on her ceiling showed up as clear and vivid as can be. Of all the holes she'd photographed, this was the one that hurt the most.

Then there was a clap of thunder. And to think I was just about to believe the lie of seasons. Then a second burst of thunder and a blinding flash of lightning. It lasted a second. She came near and stretched out her arms like a castaway pleading for help from an airplane. *Yes, Mamma, strangle me, fuck, I knew you wanted to do it, do it now, kill me, you chose the right moment.*

I closed my eyes, but the tears would not stop, and my hands were full of mauled fabric. Outside, the rain and the wind and the lightning and thunder. I squeezed my eyes shut and clenched my fists. I felt her cold wrists on my shoulders. Then her forearms. The furious rush of her arms stretching beyond my neck. Her breasts on mine. Her head behind mine. She forced her arms to close around my trembling body.

I opened my eyes.

I held her too, as hard as I could, though I couldn't stop from trembling. I cried, my nose ran all over her collarbone.

I lifted my eyes and she said the smile *Dear Camelia I told you never to do it again never talk with people promise me you won't.*

I wiped my nose with my sleeve.

"But is it ok if I keep studying Chinese?"

Only written. No more tones. No simultaneous translation from mouth to mouth. Forget about words in whatever language they come in.

The window slammed shut.

"I promise."

I didn't leave the house again. Stretched out on the couch, I watched stupid sitcoms and read the catalogs and fliers they threw against the door. The sitcoms offered a very limited inventory of keys. Especially the reruns of *Baywatch*, where the characters went to the beach during the day and drank at night, and if you consider that "beach" and "alcohol" share the same key, you can imagine the boredom of writing the same key on my skin over and over again, the same symbol on each finger. I always ended up falling asleep.

When I awoke I felt worse than before. Even the treacherous sun that had spied on me while I begged Wen to make love to me had abandoned me. In its place in the middle of the sky floated a Virgin blimp.

Meanwhile, the filth had accumulated on my mother. Not only was she not bathing, she no longer moved from the couch. She was becoming a landing pad for every kind of bug, and was seemingly proud of this role because she refused to flick off the winged monsters that shat all over her. A fashion show at Southwark Exhibition Center was showing on TV, one like she and I used to go see on the first Saturday of every month when I was fifteen. Riding the bus there we were always so excited. But my mother gave me the look called *Change channels*, as if she didn't know that the remote had been lost forever in the dusty folds of the couch.

It took a week before I forgot that it was the twenty-second of February. If you weren't careful, it would become the twenty-third, and then the twenty-fourth, and without even realizing what was happening you'd wake up in March. Even the batteries in the wall clock ran out, and I had no desire to go and buy more.

I was laying the foundations for another bout of verbal fasting, but how could I go back to silence after taking such a big step? I had committed suicide in reverse, throwing myself into life without a parachute, and down there, naturally, another goddamned hole was waiting for me.

I occasionally went to the video store to rent the Icelandic movie, but to my great disappointment I always found the Icelandic movie in the case.

*

Little by little I fell back into the fear that I had when I was little, the fear of stories.

But now it was worse: I was terrified of being dragged into some story or other, and the terror prevented me from even approaching the window and looking out. "You just have to look at people on the street," Stefano Mega would say, with his notebook in his hands. So I sewed the checkered curtains in the living room together, closing them forever.

"You know, even if you glance at another face for a second it's enough," he said, and on that unnumbered afternoon I covered the curtainless kitchen window with my ideograms.

All it takes is a passerby's glance and next thing you know you're imprisoned in somebody else's story. Or it could be a "Can you tell me where Wodehouse Street is?" or being glimpsed out of the corner of somebody's eye as they come round a corner and there you are standing at the window. Of all places! What rotten luck. What happens then is a hole opens up in the asphalt and it seizes your story and Liz Turpey's story, both guilty of turning two stories into one.

The day after the unnumbered day I turned on the TV. On the couch, my mother woke with a start. The blue hornet that had been sleeping on her shoulder flew away but found its path blocked by the window. The voice on Channel 4, such a nasally London accent that it sounded fake, was saying something about a fifteenth century minstrel by the name of Jean de la Vitte. The hornet slammed against the mummified glass for the sixth time. I know how dangerous stories can be, so I was not surprised in the least when the voice said that they'd cut out the tongue and lopped off the hands of Jean de la Vitte. The instruments of his crime.

What crime dear?

"Don't worry, Mamma. Everything's ok."

I turned off the TV. The crushed corpse of the hornet was on the floor beneath the window.

*

The days were increasingly unnumbered. Every day tried its utmost to be less numbered than the one before it. A countdown that begins at zero, gets to zero, and then zero once more, and so on until it drives you to throw yourself from Knaresborough Bridge.

One recklessly unnumbered day at a ruthlessly unspecified hour I wrapped my bedroom window in ideograms. Now nobody, not Jean de la Vitte and certainly not Wen, could take my story and torture it.

I had promised my mother that I was through with stories. I had already decided as much on the day of my father's funeral. I didn't go, neither did my mother, but the flowers made their way to us all the same; hairy heads of chrysanthemums held by human hands knocked on the door. I put the door chain on but the smell got in all the same—that allegorical smell that white flowers give off. It got inside, whole, even when my mother covered her head with a cushion, even though our mucous membranes were protected from the door by three big sacks of garbage.

A large puce carnation came headfirst through the window. What an idiot! I'd left it open.

I ran to close it and got a crucifix-shaped bouquet of red roses in the face. The business card of the florist, which specialized in funerals, said, "For a trendier mourning."

No, in my personal story I am not crazy. In my mother's, well, my mother can no longer be a part of any story because she doesn't speak and what hope does a story have these days if it doesn't have any dialogue?

After the invasion of flowers she came out from behind the cushion and said the following look: *Is it over?*

She had aged.

"Yes, Mamma, it's over. You can relax."

I ventured out to the field mined with flowers. I picked them up one by one from the asphalt. There were all kinds of floral compositions. Lilies and gladiolas. Carnations and baby's breath. Sneaks, they were, primed to deodorize our pain without our permission, for no other reason than to make everyone feel good and kind.

A heart of carnations and roses towered in the midst of a composition, and the card read: "Death does not rob us entirely of our beloved, whose works remain." Of course they remain. How could his stealth fucks disappear? I choked the lush stem of the first carnation in the line. Carnation, the word itself beautifully presaged the carnage that would cause its death.

I amputated the petals of all the flowers with my Swiss army knife, following a chromatic system of classification: first the reds, and then the pinks, and finally the whites.

Key to "color": "knife."

My mother had her head under the cushion again. I shook her and said the look, *Hey c'mon it's all clear now.*

I had a goldenrod petal on my thumbnail.

She drew a sigh called *Finally* and I accompanied her to her room.

I wanted to protect her, naturally. That's the reason I never left her, to protect her from stories. Whereas her room slowly rotted with dust and spiders and castles of mold, participating gleefully in her death, like Bluebeard's secret room.

"I will not fucking allow it!"

Outside it was daytime. While I was going on about the condolence flowers it had become even more daytime. The light sent sperm shaped halos onto the lurid windowpanes. Furiously, I tore out the thread that was holding the curtains together. The outside tumbled yellow into the room. My eyes welled with tears. After centuries of silence I spoke with my voice.

My mother covered her ears, as did Will and Grace on the television.

"Why are you looking at me like that, Mamma? Do I look crazy to you? Do you think it's crazy to want to live? You need courage, you know. You need fucking courage to talk, to leave the house! Enough! We—"

She interrupted me with the look *Why are you treating me like this?*

I was about to reply but I felt something in my throat and up came a spurt of bluish vomit, up and out onto the carpet. It said *Do you think it's crazy to want to live?* And *You need courage, you know.*

Livia shot me a look called *Look at what you've done,* pointing at the vomit.

I put on my leather jacket with the twin holes in it and went out.

God, so much light.

It was annoyingly warm outside, the flowers threw open their petals loosely beneath the sizzling kisses of an unfettered sun.

The gray wool dress with the mismatched sleeves felt heavy on me, it released a schizophrenic sweat: boiling hot on my chest and thighs, and a pandemonium of chills on my arms.

Yep, it must have been March all right. Terrifyingly March.

I went back in. It was December in there, of course. I got my yellow dress, the one suffering from an outbreak of canvas patches, and I cut off the sleeves and half of the skirt, then I dropped the neckline to the level of my breasts. I put it on. I went to look at myself in the bathroom mirror. A concoction of toothpaste and breath climbed the mirror and split it in half.

There were two gigantic green eyes.

There was a sunken face with gravediggers' shovels hanging from its eyes.

There was a big nose.

Not enormous, but you'd definitely find it on Google Maps.

There was a mouth. There was my full one meter and sixty centimeters summarized out of spite in the sixty centimeters of the mirror.

There was hair.

My hair, woefully straight most of the time, was now bouncing on my shoulders in gay little waves, and out of its dull black color had wriggled a black as shiny and spry as ink on which a lascivious zigzagging light faded. And what to say of my split ends! They had mysteriously gathered into a single univocal curl of energy and healthfulness.

I brushed feverishly for ten minutes but my hair would not yield, not even the dancing ringlets that my bangs had become.

I left the house.

I walked to the shop through a light that was greedy and noisy like a cat in heat.

I walked and sweated. I passed the gas station, the florist . . . Seeing them there was a pleasure, those flowers with the mutilated roots, prostituting their prissy perfumes. It was a joy to see the hands of the florist, who, like some pimp, chose the prettiest roses, lumped them all together, and squeezed the stems into coarse aluminum foil girdles.

Then he said, "Here you are," and he gave them to a boy in a tracksuit. Maybe they were for his wife. What am I saying? They were for his lover, of course. And even as he was getting into his car he couldn't help but bury his nose in the damp, red petals, close his eyes, and smile. He was smiling because he had a lover and his wife didn't know; he was smiling because I, on the other hand, had been rejected by a piece of shit who had led me on.

He was smiling because he still didn't know that there was a hole waiting for him on Grosvenor Road, and that even if he were the one to die in that hole, it would be his daughter who suffered the most.

Do not allow children near the porthole.

If I had known that the most I could hope for was suffering on an installment plan, suffering that would be reborn promptly three years after the fact thanks to something as stupid as unrequited love, I would have killed myself first.

I watched the boy in his Lonsdale tracksuit and his male pattern balding, I saw him turn on the engine, his nose was still buried deep in the red curves of the petals, the rose spiraling open beneath the voracious sniff of nostrils; false rose, betrayer, mutilated whore.

The shop was open.

I went in. There was nobody there. I said, "Hello," in the strange voice people use when they're talking to themselves. I looked around. Nothing but clothes. The same clothes that had witnessed my arrival every Tuesday and Thursday for my lesson with Wen. The same clothes that saw me implore him to make love to me.

Colored clothes, clothes with stripes, shiny symmetrical buttons, sassy little love hearts, cheering little stars, languid lace frills, tight-fitting promises of a fantastic weekend, shiny nylon that frees the world of its sins.

The clothes had multiplied over the course of a month.

I ran my fingers along the lying false silk of the nightshirts, I scrunched up the frills sewn on machines.

A plague of synthetic gracefulness.

With frequent outbreaks of compulsive youthfulness.

And a high risk of eternally requited love side effects.

Three years ago I would have liked this shop so much.

I took the scissors from the drawer behind the counter. I pounced on a pair of pink overalls at the head of a row, disemboweling that frivolous head of the class, which I imagined being that of an agonizingly obliging blond Englishwoman.

The shoulder straps were the first to fall, like a cheerleader's pom-poms. Then my snips became more imaginative, holes the shape of sexual organs, for example, and now it was the checked miniskirt's turn; she was so shit scared she was losing threads all over the place, but I showed no remorse. My fabric genocide became increasingly bloody as I worked my way down the row from S to XL. No survivors.

My weapons included wire from the coat hangers, which I used to strangle the shirt collars. But I also transformed them into the birdcages to be fitted to one's breasts. They are worn two sizes smaller than your usual size because they have to squeeze you until you bleed. That way you lose the desire to have you breasts licked by your Italian lover.

There! Another strike to the shoulder of the nylon blouse, the one hiding behind the faux velour dress, that innocent yellow nylon blouse stricken with daisies. They must all be snipped, from the "S" for savage sodomy to the "M" for murder, morbid, monster, misery, and Mamma.

My hands were shaking but I continued to amputate. The black sleeves of a cotton dress that had been made for hugging would never be fulfilled; they would hug the floor, a lump of gangrenous severed fabric. I admired the perfectly spherical porthole I had just given a jacket. "Do not allow children near the porthole," I said.

A voice replied, "I'm calling the police."

"No, no. Wait."

It was he. The brother who lived in the back. He looked at me with his stupid surprised eyes. He was wearing a T-shirt the color of rotting leaves with the words "Sweet memories moonlight friends" printed on it. His long red mouth opened to talk over me, then it opened some more, grew even longer, and he held it agape until it looked like a woman giving birth, and repeated, "I'm calling the police."

"I'll reimburse you for everything."

"I'm calling the police."

"No, fuck off, wait. I'll pay everything back. Where's Wen?"

"He's not here."

"What do you mean he's not here?"

"I'm here on Wednesdays. You're his girlfriend, right?"

"No."

"He had no shirt on."

"Why were you spying on us?"

"I wasn't spying on you, I had to tell him something."

He dragged his hands back and forth in the air when he spoke.

"Then why did you just stand there?"

"Don't be mean to me."

"I'm not being mean!"

"Your tone of voice isn't nice. Give me the money you owe me and get out of my shop."

"You're so rude."

"You're the one who ruined the clothes."

"Wen says you do the same thing. Here, this is all the money I have. I'll bring you more tomorrow. I needed to do this."

"Take your dress off."

"Sorry, what did you say?"

"You stole it from here."

"I didn't. I pulled it out of the dumpster, I didn't steal it!"

"But I'm taking it back now."

"What are you, retarded? I'm leaving, ciao."

He looked at me, his eyes burning with a strange insolence.

"Wait, don't go. One thing."

I turned.

"You're beautiful."

"Huh? No, I'm not beautiful at all, what rubbish."

"Your eyes are green."

"Yes, like mold."

I left. The warm air seized my thighs. I started walking. It's not hard: I go back to my mother, I go home, and, as always, switch on the TV, and give her a shower. But I was sweating, I was soaked. I walked past the church and the supermarket, and the wall that hid the green foliage.

It's not hard: I go back. Back to being the bodyguard of my own sadness, back to my mother, back home, to the nature reserve of my fetid memories. I stopped at the pharmacy and turned around. He was sitting behind the cash register when I entered the shop.

"Here, you're right. Take your dress."

I took off the dress and walked towards him in my underwear. His eyes popped open. He had a nice lean body, he was tall with long legs and a narrow nose like his brother's. That is, in that obscure expression of his there was a mixed-up chance at beauty. You had to concentrate to see it; you had to suck it out of the white lagoon of his witless face.

I crouched down beneath the table and unbuttoned his old high-waisted jeans. I breathed in the smell of cheap bath soap. I moved my head towards his briefs as if I were slamming it against a wall.

He was trying to say something but he couldn't. I saw his chest inflate as he drew a breath to speak. The words rose in his throat and pushed his wide, thin red lips apart. Then they lost all substance, became a sigh, his breath quickened.

Back and forth I went, filling myself with him, with the words he couldn't say, with the words Wen would never say to me, and they had a rubbery taste.

I continued as the sun perspired all over me. He opened his mouth. More words that became sighs, moans, ever closer to a cry, his eyes became slits, then he closed them completely, his mouth like a vulgar crescent moon that is too close to the earth.

A gust of wind made the red cat jingle. I turned. The cat looked like a hanging corpse. I returned to Jimmy's briefs, I stared into his eyes, and seconds later he flooded my throat.

He threw his head back and wrapped his legs around me. "Thank you," he said. "Thank you, my brother's girlfriend."

When I got home it was almost dinnertime and my mother was sleeping on the couch. She must have been sleeping there all day, without waking up that morning; the builders across the street hadn't disturbed her, or the airplane that had flown low over Headingley an hour earlier. I looked at the long arc that her arm traced, a taut white arc, an arc that was the synthesis of all geometry. I looked at her mouth; her bottom lip protruded slightly. It used to make me think that she always had something to say, but then that mouth was virgin again.

I looked at the complexity of the folds that formed in the tracksuit around her breasts, which were no longer able to hold themselves up. I imagined myself reading those folds like you read lifelines on someone's palm.

I looked at the round bone of her ankle and the meaty urgency of the veins on her feet. I thought about all the waste that woman was accumulating, the waste of body and mind, of days, of her existence, and I knew that deep inside she must have gotten some pleasure out of it, and out of making me part of the waste.

I felt my head fill with white heat. I picked up the photos she had taken of a hole in a tablecloth and ran off to look for the others that she kept in her room. The stink of urine, sweat, old wood, stale air, and chips imploded between the gray walls of her room like compressed air. I went to open the window. It didn't open. Holding my nose, I slalomed between dirty underwear strewn on the floor and supermarket fliers. I found thirty-nine photos.

I collected holes of every type. They disgusted me. I threw them in the wheelie bin in front of our house. Then I picked up a supermarket flier and cut out four large purplish apples, six long glossy bananas, and two brightly colored rubber dog toys—the ones that make noise—and two large red dresses for pregnant women.

First, I locked her Polaroid in the room that contained all the hurtful objects, my father's room.

Then I stuck the images on the living room wall with the ideograms. And that's not all: in the corner of each image I scribbled its key, that way there would be no confusion.

*

When my mother saw the images and the Chinese keys written all over them she stood up with a verve that I hadn't seen in her in years and tore them down. She was in a frenzy. The last time I had seen her move that way, she was still working at the radio. She danced and my father laughed happily. We had just moved here. He'd been offered a job at the *Leeds Daily*. These days, when someone on the street waves a copy in my face and cries, "*Leeds Daily*, please!" it takes all my strength not to strangle them.

My mother kept on pulling the images down, and when she had finished she collapsed on the couch and closed her eyes.

Look, Papa, look at your wife, look at the rotten fruit of your death.

I hated him with unbelievable intensity. Not because he had betrayed my mother, or because his betrayal had killed him and deprived me of a father, but because he had died once, and once only, whereas I died every day, and she did too.

"C'mon, Mamma, let's go now and have a shower."

She looked confused. Then she lowered her eyelids, stretched her legs out over the filthy, faded cushions, opened her eyes again, and stared at me. Sadistic wrinkles stretched her eyes all the way to her temples, to where her hair began. They extended her gaze; in fact, she saw more than most, I'm sure of it. She saw all the horrible things that are hiding in the void, that will leap out of ditches and ambush you.

I stabbed the arm of the couch with my pen, nine inky wounds that together formed the ideogram "hate." At the base of the ideogram there's a beating heart that is nothing like the foolish hearts that one draws but resembles a real one, flaccid and oozing, furiously pumping life to one's brain. And at the top is night. And nearby there's someone turning around.

Even my mother turned around and saw nothing, neither the heart nor the night, and her gaze returned to a dumb point in the floor. God, she used to be beautiful. Everyone said she looked like Cate Blanchett: high cheekbones, a narrow nose, I remember it all. I remember her beautiful, as she was when she was alive, when she was really alive.

I remember the quickened wheat of her hair, the honest blue of her eyes. I used to look at her from below as one looks at statues, and I continued to look at her from below, because I never outgrew my father's five feet three inches. My hair too, was the same rat-black color as his, but my mother told me I was beautiful, my mother told me many things a long time ago.

He even got the better of beauty, because he was short, with a prominent nose, but then his ugliness stopped where it was forever, no wrinkles marred the face in the newspaper. But my mother's beauty crumpled and drooped like a poster.

But beauty is not the point anymore. These days, thinking about beauty in my house is like betting on a horse whose intestines are hanging out. These days, if you so much as say the word beauty, a sterile rain falls that disinfects your mouth. These days, if beauty walks down Christopher Road, she's sure to get stabbed.

I went to give my mother a kiss, but instead I ran to my room.

Who knows if you'd think she looks like Cate Blanchett if you saw her now.

The next day I woke up, put on my white dress full of buttons in the most improbable places, and went to the shop.

There it is, the human road sign saying, "Run away from here." There he is in all the stillness that made me fall in love with him. There he is showing surprise at seeing me and hiding his gaze in the floor, and then with his limp hands he waves at me, but only to remind me that once upon a time he managed to escape, once, when my hand attempted to unbutton his trousers.

If he hadn't rejected me that day, if he had been his typically submissive self and let me unbutton his jeans and undress him, making escape impossible, he would have failed miserably in his role as exit sign man.

Because it is the exception to the rule that maketh the exit sign man. For his perpetual suspended-leg immobility to be credible he must, every now and again, escape. If not, who on earth would ever run in his direction?

You need ruthless talent to be the exit sign man. But it is easy to be his victim, you just have to find his wares in the garbage, pull them out, and in a heartbeat you find yourself with your head bent over his shabby jeans and your brain riddled with love lymphoma.

"Are you still angry at me, Camelia. Because, you know, I—"

"No."

"I knew you'd understand. I'm going to get the Chinese book! I knew you'd come back. I have a present for you."

He disappeared for a moment behind the counter, and pulled out a red bag.

"It was my mother's."

I took it from him. It was a Chinese-English dictionary from 1945.

"There's something special, look at the second page."

"'List of characters with obscure keys.'"

"Fun, right?"

"It's nice."

That's how I started back at Chinese lessons. I didn't expect it to happen. He told me that in September there was an exam that I could sit, one of those officially recognized exams that give you a certificate when you finish. So he started giving me more and more homework, and I attended lessons more frequently.

"And these are the resultative verbs."

"What does that mean?"

"That the verb you want to use is the result of two sequential verbs. For example, look at this, 'to learn' is written by combining 'to study-to be able,' because if you are able to study you've learned."

As I was returning home I forgot to return home.

My legs kept on walking, and I found myself in the center of town in that magic moment in which all the shops shut their gaping iron mouths. The owners pull them down with relief, hungry, no doubt, for pudding and all that other rubbish they eat here. The sun set with its habitual gentlemanly ease, but everyone knows that as soon as gentlemen get inside a pub they start belching and vomiting all over the waitresses.

I turned into one of the cross streets, there was a bookstore open with a English-Leeds English bilingual dictionary in the window, and then a little colorful shop with a neon sign saying, "Tattoos for all." I thought it sounded like some kind of obligatory and bloody branding, like the numbers seared onto people's arms in the concentration camps. When I got back to the main street it was cold and a strong wind was blowing. I had goose bumps and I held my arms over my chest and rubbed them to keep warm, I rubbed them all the way along Briggate as it emptied of people and grew darker and darker, becoming the unsettling and vague street of dreams, those dreams in which you're naked and you don't know how to get home, and there's a neon sign calling you, and a club shining bright red in the middle of all that darkness, the only bright spot, like the infected eye of a Cyclops, and inside I knew that there were people rubbing up against other people. I rubbed until I perceived some feeling in my skin, until I could feel the energy coming from my pores and the resistance mounted by my arm hairs. I was already standing in front of Morrisons and my fingertips exuded heat, communicating with my muscles, with my bones, searching for something, a Chinese character with its unequivocal key, and I told myself, yes, I desire an ideographic life sentence, I will tattoo myself with a Chinese word, black as any hell that is not Leeds, I decided, and between my legs I felt a sudden vulnerability.

It was Wednesday, March. It'd be too hard to say which day in March (give me time). I went to the shop. Jimmy was sewing a sleeve onto the front of a pink shirt with white flowers. He was wearing a violet shirt that sported the words "Fooly cooly cola party."

"What the hell are you doing?"

He ran towards me like an enormous baby. He hugged me hard.

"Hi, my brother's girlfriend!"

"You shouldn't be here, Jimmy."

"Why?"

"Don't make that face."

"My brother's not here, let's go."

"Go where?"

"I don't know."

He hugged me. I felt my bones collapse like a matchstick castle. I unhooked his hands. A Post-it with the ideogram "to dare" on it fell out of my sweat-soaked pocket onto the floor.

I hugged him back. I grabbed the shirt with the extra sleeve and stuffed it in my Invicta backpack. I held tightly to Jimmy's long, damp palm.

Some things begin with a hole, like trees—you dig a hole in the earth to make a place for them in the universe. Babies, too, grow in a hole, and come out of one. One mustn't forget that. I was reminded when Wen gave me the 1945 dictionary. That evening, thumbing through it, I came across the word "hole" and I discovered that its key was "baby."

Other things, however, begin with a train. Jimmy and I decided to take one to Scarborough. I sat next to a blond child who was singing a song I didn't understand as I watched Jimmy waiting to buy tickets. I watched him, a tall Chinese boy with incredibly long hands and a gray pile vest over a violet sweater gesticulating at the ticket seller, tracing a large half-moon with his arm as if performing a magic trick as he pulled a few bills out of his pocket. I watched him as he came towards me in his strange cartoon character frenzy and as he opened his remarkably wide mouth and said: "All done!"

There were all kinds of people on the train saying all kinds of words to each other. I had an impulse to write the keys to every word I heard. But the words were faster than my wrist, they moved at the speed of light, or nearly. So I gave up and turned to Jimmy.

"Jimmy, you're not retarded, right?"

"Did my brother tell you that?"

"Yes."

"He says that because of the clothes."

"Come to think of it, why do you do that to those clothes?"

"I ruin them just to spite him."

"Really? Why?"

Gesticulating hysterically, he pulled a comic book out of his backpack. He started to read. On the cover, underneath a grotesque laughing face and a hand holding a hammer, were swelling red letters written in the angular alphabet that the Japanese use for foreign words. And then the translation into Chinese.

"Jimmy?"

He didn't answer. His eyes followed the panels. Every now and then he laughed with his extra large mouth. His gums red and slimy like raw meat.

I turned to the window.

Houses dotting open fields, each one different from the last, high and low, pitched roofs and flat ones, dark brown or cherry red, camel orange with brown sheds, the color of sand shot through with black. Only the windows were the same, always, white with white curtains, and closed, all of them. A trace of humanity in the window would have been unpardonably gauche.

They shot past, those houses. They became specters lacking outlines, misshapen visions. The color flaked off them and mixed with the knots of smoke coming from the chimneys, becoming all the colors of the universe.

They were too beautiful, those houses, to be still allowing death to dwell on them.

"Go on, Jimmy, tell my why you ruin the clothes?"

He lifted his long totem head.

"Look, Camelia, horses! I like the white one."

The month that began that day—although it was already the twelfth, as was revealed to me by the electronic oracle on Jimmy's wrist—was such a strange and exciting March that I can't even call it March. It must have a virgin name, a firsthand one, one that nobody has ever pronounced before.

A name that when spoken aloud covered me again with the odor of scorched earth stretching along the road and then hiding in the strong smell of the ocean. And something else: a threatening odor from below, the stink of fried fish and also gasoline, but then all odors led to a single odor, the smell of Jimmy's semen.

"I feel like laughing, Camelia, you know?"

"Why?"

"Because you're special fantastic super special."

"Hm."

"My life is more wonderful now."

The sea was flat and transparent, and on the sand a tight row of green, white, and brown houses, all different heights, one stuck to the other, an orgy of bricks that stuck out, breathless, over the shoreline. At houses' end, a white lighthouse in the distance.

I looked at Jimmy, at the consistency of his knuckles on those kilometer-long fingers. When somewhere in the world some idiot says to his girlfriend, "I'd steal the moon for you," he should know that there really is someone whose fingers are long enough to do it. But it's not the moon I want.

Jimmy sat on the sand and I sat next to him. He touched my hair in an absurd way, as if he were ridding me of fleas.

"Do you like me a lot, Camelia?"

"It's complicated."

"What's complicated?"

"Forget about it."

"Come with me to a special place?"

"Where?"

"Come."

He took off his clothes and stood there in his swimming costume. I did the same. I followed him along the beach until there were no more people and all you could hear was the puffing and chugging of the sea. He dove in and I followed. The water was freezing, it woke every bone in my body. I stared down at the gaping underwater abysses, the darkly darting fish, the web of light that moved on the rocks bringing them brutally to life. Everything escaped stillness, everything, even the discolored coins slipped occasionally from one rock to another, you just had to watch, but I stopped for a moment and there was no air, help! I jumped out of the water afraid for my life.

Jimmy swam ten or so meters away from me, his long gangly arms striking the water without rhyme or reason. He turned back to face me, around him a forty carat light glimmered and just looking at it made you feel poor and needy.

"What are you doing, Camelia? Come on."

I reached him swimming freestyle. He stopped at a tiny sheltered inlet formed out of rock, like a small cave. It was big enough for the two of us, but there was no room for anything else. In the middle, though, there was a funnel-shaped hole and if you drew near it roared at you.

"Is here ok?"

"It's a little tight, Jimmy."

His mega-mouth lifted into a smile.

"Lie down."

"But the hole—"

"Go on, lie down, it's not like we're going to fall into it."

So I lay down. He did too, on top of me. The hole to our left. It made the sound of the sea only deeper. The ocean's throat clogged with rubbers and Coca-Cola cans.

He started kissing me. He was like a dog eating from a bowl—brutal frenzied movements, his teeth playing swords with mine. It was one big clamorous clang. I opened my eyes, he had three, like a giant alien licking my soul.

"You're beautiful, my brother's girlfriend."

"My name is Camelia."

"You're beautiful, Camelia!"

The water ran over me, living threads of matter becoming black on my bikini.

During wash cycles the transparent porthole tends to heat up.

Jimmy in his swim trunks, the words "sporty bunny posse" written on them. Jimmy and the excited threat of his body, his rapid breathing, the spread of his hips, Jimmy Largemouth, his liquid eyes and Donald Duck gestures. His infinite hands spreading my legs.

"Opening the porthole and placing clothes in."

"The porthole opens."

"Before placing clothes inside, make sure that there are no animal remains left in the drum."

"Spread the clothes out evenly inside the drum."

"You're so beautiful, yes, yes."

The sun, fleshy like a chicken breast, poked into the cave, withdrew, and then came back. Fried chicken from McDonald's—buy some and you get my body free.

Then, the end.

"Remove clothes. End of cycle. The water will drain."

His water spilled on a rock but for one splash on my knee. The following sound indicates that the cycle has finished: "Camelia, it was wonderful."

"Yes, Jimmy. It was for me too."

He was breathing hard, his eyes half-closed. He laid himself on the ground, his exhausted body, shimmering and alive like a city, with all the architectural complexity of his bones, the ancient mountains of his shoulder blades, the ocean swell of his chest that rose with each breath, everything was there, including me, my secret rivers.

The sea gargled crazily in the hole.

I took his hand.

"What is it, Camelia?"

"Can I write something on you, here?"

"How, you've got no pen?"

"With my finger."

"It tickles!"

"Finished. It's an ideogram that I invented earlier today. A new ideogram that's all mine. From this moment on it means, 'Water is always running, it is the same water that is in a mother's womb and also that same water your poured in me, it is life.'"

"I don't understand you at all. You're beautiful, Camelia, but you're a bit strange."

"Why? I can't invent ideograms? It has a precise meaning, look! I included the character for 'equal' plus the key for 'water,' so it becomes 'the same water . . . ' Don't you like it?"

I was terribly excited. But he wouldn't even look at me anymore. The sun fell into his enormous eyes but he remained impassive like one of those terra-cotta warriors in Xi'an.

"Let's head back to Leeds, Jimmy?"

"Hm."

Aristotle was right: man is a social animal. In fact, when he wasn't being social Jimmy was only an animal. I stood and jumped into the water.

It was six-thirty when I got home. My mother was sleeping on the couch, buried beneath pictures of holes in a belt. I picked up the broom and the dustpan, and set about sweeping and cleaning the house. I rubbed the gray halos off the windows, I chased the spiders away and demolished their homes. I crushed every conspiracy of dust beneath the couch.

Then I woke my mother, wiped the potato chip crumbs from her mouth, and led her to the bathroom. I pushed her under the shower, and, with her old ragged sponge, I sandpapered the brown spots that encircled her neck like some grotesque noose. I rinsed her, soaped her up again, and rinsed again. During the wash cycle the porthole tends to heat up.

"How do you get so dirty?"

She answered with the look *No-how-do-you-stay-so-clean.*

As I dried her a shameful feeling of annoyance rose to my head. I looked at her and that obtuse grimace on her face became a self-satisfied smile. Self-satisfied because I was the one who cleaned her, washed her, prepared her meals, while she sat like some omniscient god on the couch, ahead of me, on high, beyond language.

And from down there the world had to rise towards her, serve her, and sympathize with her . . . "You know what, Mamma, you can fucking dry yourself."

She replied with a look whose meaning I no longer remembered. I left her in the bathroom wrapped in pink terry toweling.

Key to "punish": "heart."

Tuesday, March eighteenth at six-ten, Wen was biting the nails of one hand and writing with the other, wrapped in his yellow zippered sweater that was at least two sizes too big for him.

To his right, there were two eggs submerged in tea.

"And this is another potential . . . Are you listening, Camelia?"

"Yes, of course, but I don't understand."

"What don't you understand?"

"Why potential? What has potency got to do with anything?"

"You're obsessed with the names of things."

"No, it's just that I don't understand what they're for."

"Read this paragraph. They 'indicate the possibility or impossibility that the action described takes place and that a result occurs, or that the action described takes places in the intended direction.'"

"Meaning?"

"Look at this sentence again: *ni haohaor de ciangxiang, yiding xiang de qilai.*"

"It means, 'If you think about it, it will come to mind.' Right?"

"Yes, right. So you see the potential 'come to mind' is formed by combining 'to think,' 'to rise,' and 'to come.' It's the movement of the thought that comes to your mind suddenly, get it?"

"Yes, more or less. Can I do one?"

"What?"

"Make a potential."

"Sorry, Camelia, but you can't just invent potentials."

"Why not?"

"Because you can't . . . "

"Listen! For example, if I put the participle between the word 'break' and 'rocks' it would mean the movement of the waves, right?"

"No, Camelia, you can't do that."

"And what about between two people, if you put the participle between two people, what movement do they make?"

"I don't know what you mean . . . Shall we go to dinner?"

"What do you mean?"

"Aren't you hungry?"

"Yes, a lot."

I smiled.

Wen disappeared behind the red door. Was Jimmy back there, too? Who knows.

I imagined a room with red carpet, a red ceiling, rice paper colored walls full of corpulent red ideograms like those done by calligraphers, the brush strokes flitting and fluid like fish and the color intact until the very end where it dies suddenly, without any mingy dribbles of ink.

A wave of heat washed over my entire body and exploded in my groin.

Wen came out of the red room dressed to the nines. Beautiful. Mine.

We went out, he closed the store.

We walked slowly until the cemetery came to greet us. Headingley was already sleeping, an expanse of nameless headstones was its flesh. It slept like an exhausted god, stretched out on its belly in the cemetery, hidden amidst death, ready to leap on someone and bring him back to life.

And we walked over him, in silence, excited. We opened the gate, we surrounded the dead, we spoke all over the headstones in our furtive Chinese. A slaughter of tones and reflexive consonants, of guttural projectiles, invisible ideograms hidden in every word, each one with its sharpened key, each one with its own meaning, with its invulnerable morphosyllabicity.

Him: "The sky is so black!"

Me: "*Tian zheme hei!*"

Him: "It might rain tomorrow."

Me: "*Mingtian keneng xia yu.*"

And so on, one sentence after another, one on top of the other, to slay death itself, to slay everything that was unable to clear the customs house of our vocal cords, everything that we could not translate.

Him: "I like places like this."

Me: "*Wo xihuan zheyang de difang.*"
Him: "Are you hungry?"
Me: "*Ni e ma?*"
And then: "Yes, I'm hungry."
My heart was beating hard, I felt it in my throat and in the webbing between my fingers, and in my hair and in my shoulder bag. There was nothing but my heart, the rest of my body was light and inconsistent, something the wind could have its way with, like a paper person in one of those paper people chains that kindergarteners make.
Him: "There's no moon."
Me: "*Yueliang bu zai.*"
"No, you say *mei you yueliang.*"
"But that means, 'I don't have the moon.'"
"I've explained it before, that's how you say it."

The gate swung shut behind us. A ridiculous question occurred to me: "He doesn't want to eat at my place, does he?" But then we turned and after about a hundred meters we came to a restaurant. Four red ideograms, bright and puffy, embossed on a shingle and above them the transcription: *Kongzi fandian*, the restaurant of Confucius.

I had never seen such an immaculate Chinese restaurant, let alone imagined one could be found there, in such an ugly neighborhood, mine, that is. The tables were separated by walnut dividers carved with images of dragons; the red paper lanterns hung low over the tables and cast a precious light; the waitresses' satin dresses were blinding. I felt underdressed in my jeans and sweater, both with their ink-stained pajama pocket appendages. Wen was wearing a coat and tie. He made quite a strange impression with his hair gelled back and all the diminutive symmetrical lines of his face bared.

He gestured to the cook, who disappeared for a minute and came back with a wooden cart and a plump glazed duck. He ceremoniously carved it in front of us tracing wide arcs in the air with the knife like he was illustrating some philosophical principle or the rudiments of some martial art that had not yet been rendered banal by Westerners.

"Nice restaurant, Wen. How did you find it?"

"My ex-student brought me here."

"Oh look, the waitress is coming with our fried lotus petals."

"I wonder how fried Camelia petals taste, eh?"

"Why is your face so serious when you make jokes?"

"Sorry, it's my face."

The Chinese girl leaned over the table and placed the plate at its center. It made a strange impression on me to see her ample bosom, uncommon among Chinese women, compressed painfully in her dress. I thought about my father's round face buried in the bosom of his lover, there on Grosvenor Road. The thought carried fresh pain with it, a light one, like a pain based on my pain but featuring a jazzy soundtrack and a couple of Oscar-winning actors.

"I really want to do something, Wen."

"What?"

"I don't know. Something fun. Something fun with you. Tonight. Do you have any ideas?"

"Well, maybe we could see a Chinese movie, so you can practice."

"What do you have?"

"I have a really good one called *The Hole*, by Cai Mingliang."

"What's it about?"

"A boy and girl who communicate through a hole that has formed in her ceiling, which, you know, is also his floor."

"And do they meet?"

"No."

"What! They live in the same building one floor away and they never meet."

"No. Do you want some more Qingdao beer?"

"Yes. Can we watch it at your shop? I mean, sorry, you're not going back to Knaresborough tonight, are you?"

"No."

"No what?"

"Yes, sorry, I mean we can watch it at the shop."

After dinner we went out into the freezing cold street. My fingers burned and throbbed inside my pockets. There was nobody around. We walked quickly, single file into the maw of the frigid moonless night, as if walking was nothing more than a way of warming up.

We came out on Woodhouse Street. It was deserted, even though the neon signs insisted on bleating food of every color.

"Wen, I'm glad we're going to watch a movie."

He gave me a thin smile without looking at me. I thought back to Knaresborough and decided that Woodhouse Street was another place that had only us.

Then there's Headingley that has only us.

And the abandoned church that has only us.

Wen's dark shop that has only us.

The minute we got to it, I stopped, full of surprise and gratitude.

I couldn't believe it. It was a miracle that even to get a place where we would sit near to each other we just needed to walk.

"Hey, Wen, in the dark doesn't it seem like a temple? I've seen them on the Internet, Buddhist temples . . . "

Him looking for the key in his red parka, me imagining the cold of the metal meeting the cold of his fingers. He turned the key in the lock.

"Hey, Wen, does it have subtitles? No worries if it doesn't, I'll watch it anyway. It's not as cold now, right?"

He turned to face me, his small nose and high arched nostrils, his eyebrows like commas written by a child, and his eyes on the ground with men's shoes and dogs' needs.

"Wen?"

His luminous face like a bar sign to someone dying of thirst.

"Sorry, Camelia, I'm tired. Is it ok if I accompany you home?"

He approached me, stepping out of the streetlamp's light. He was no longer luminous. No longer a bar sign. And if you're thirsty, you can drink your own fucking piss.

"I can get home alone. Ciao."

"No, wait. Sorry, I can accompany you."

I turned and started walking.

The road was longer now, and colder, and darker, and the walls were higher, the houses behind them were farther away and finer. I couldn't bring myself to turn around to see if he was following me or if that silence was silence or the silent sound of his steps in worn rubber soles that you can never hear.

I got to the cemetery and it was more alive than I was, every headstone was a bacchanalia of fanciful shadows, and it was laughing, drunk on death, laughing with the sound of owls, laughing at people like me who were still alive and didn't know how the hell it happened.

Jesus, I wanted to turn around and look behind me, but my legs kept on moving, mysteriously, like the severed heads of men condemned to death in the Middle Ages.

I turned around.

Nobody was there.

At home I took off my sweater and jeans and laid them out on the operating table of my desk. Who knows what my mother was up to while I was eating at the Chinese restaurant and hoping and smiling like a fool. While I was deciding that my life would be incomplete without a second cocktail of humiliation and pain with leftover yearning for suicide. While I was suffering as I have suffered ever since, at God's behest, the light cast out the darkness.

She won't have eaten. Won't have washed. Won't have lifted

her head off the cushion. If I stopped caring for her, would she croak so easily? It's incredible.

I looked at the clothes. I began with the sweater that Wen had not taken off me today and continued with the jeans that he hadn't unbuttoned.

Through the window, behind the grease and the dust and other mysterious stains, the sky opened like stage curtains on another perverse hailstorm.

I picked up the scissors and sent the blue sweater to 70% acrylic 30% wool hell. I amputated cleanly the whole part that hid the breasts that Wen will never want to see. What is there to see anyway, my bosom is an A at the most.

And if you count to three, my love . . . Only three short years later . . .

One, two, three . . . But I already know what happens.

You do? You already know?

Yes, I'll still have the breasts of a child.

A child waiting for her papa while, far from here, he is fucking someone. A child whose pocket-sized Chinese lover doesn't want her.

I pulled the ideograms off the wall one by one. I sewed them onto the holes, prostheses of meaning. By the time the hail stopped, over my breast I had sewn four strokes that meant "No," which one pronounces "Boo," like when a ghost jumps out from the shadows with its arms outstretched and gives you a heart attack.

In place of my arms the sentence: "It's impossible."

I laughed. I cried.

I threatened my eye sockets with the scissors: *Just you try to weep again.*

Just try to make me believe that it's beauty I'm searching for, like I'm so banal. Beauty is out there, it's everywhere. God made it in six days and there it sits, it hasn't budged since. It's in everything that grows around you without ever asking you permission. But ugliness needs man to bring it about, to force it on the world. It's a distortion of the cosmic order. You need man to shoot concrete all over the gardenias.

Ugliness is more human. It's power. It's a true story without a moral that starts with my scissors and ends with the acrylic that is flowering on all those lucky garments.

Ugliness is a ghetto in my room on the first floor. Ugliness is my genes selling my soul to the devil and sending the proceeds to UNICEF orphans.

My mobile phone beeped. It was a text from Jimmy.

A series of empty squares.

A crossword puzzle.

"Jimmy, I can't read Chinese characters on my phone," I wrote.

Him: "I said tomorrow Scarborough again, ok?"

I amputated the left leg of the jeans without anesthesia. I hung it on the wall with a single nail like a Cyclops.

"Of course I'll come to Scarborough, we can swim together until we drown."

Him: "You're beautiful and when I think of you I touch myself all day."

Wednesday, March nineteenth: as I was making coffee my mother came into the kitchen naked.

A bestial nudity, like you see in documentaries. She molested the space with her presence, and you half expected her to spring at you prompted by some atavistic hunger.

She moved towards the steel cupboard doors above the sink and began looking for the cereal with her long, bony hands.

She turned to face me: Livia Mega on the Discovery Channel. Me running to escape her jaws. The English changing channels.

"Mamma, what the fuck?"

Her body coming towards me. The shameful bareness of her veins, turgid blue sentences carved into her legs, and the nakedness of her bones, minuscule necropoli protruding from her neck, her torso, and around the flaccid dunes of her breasts.

And her areola—grimy marks sticking out like a cow's tits. *Needy* like those of a cow.

"Mamma, shame on you, go get dressed!"

She replied with the look, *Shame on you not only have you started talking again but now you're making love to a boy you don't love and not even telling the one you do love about it.*

"What? How dare you? Mind your own fucking business. And what the hell do you know about love, about sex? What could you possibly know anymore, now that you're nothing more than a houseplant? Huh? You know what you're going to do now, Mamma? You're going to leave the house!"

I swept the coffeemaker off the table. My mother groaned as the metal body slid across the kitchen tiles and came to a stop. Black liquid oozed from the spout.

I ran into my room. Turned on the computer. Searched "photography course."

I clicked "Apply online."

I wrote everything down on a piece of paper. The street and the number. Details of the course. The things to bring to lessons. The teacher's introduction. I made a superhuman effort not to copy down all the names of last year's students.

I went downstairs and shoved the paper between her fingers.

"Look, Mamma, I signed you up, it's twice a week, I'm going to make you go to every lesson, you got it or not?"

Whatever look she replied, I was not interested.

I left the house.

Right in front of the cemetery I came across a foolhardy platoon of fuchsias. All that chlorophyll, all that wind on petals, that unnerving wait before they could open beneath the stingy Leeds sun, when it would have been easier to send a kid to Christopher Road to finish me off with a knife.

At that hour in the center of town it was pleasantly cool, and above all there were few people around.

Jimmy was standing waiting for me in front of the station, when he saw me he came bounding up to me like a cocker spaniel. He was wearing a shirt that read, "If I reborn I am California party hero." Underneath, there were some Chinese characters. He hugged me hard, too hard. The petals of the martyred fuchsia fell from my fist.

"I thought you'd never get here."

"Yes, I know, I'm late."

"No, no, don't worry. You're beautiful."

"Sure I am. My hair is filthy! Come on, let's get our tickets."

"Got them," he said with a little laugh as he pulled them out of his pocket like a rabbit from a hat.

On board the train I enjoyed the mad dash of the countryside. Fields, fields, sheep. Then a ribbon of red houses.

The sun rose with me, it rose because I was watching it. It harvested all the green of the fields and the white of the sheep.

"Jimmy."

"What is it?"

"Do you remember in that movie by Zhang Yimou when the calligraphy school is stormed and everyone decides to continue writing ideograms rather than escape even as the arrows hit them and they die?"

"I don't watch movies."

"Really? And what do you do all day?"

"Look over there!"

"What is it?"

"Sheep with blue marks on them. Why do they paint them?"

"To tell them apart, I think."

"I like the red ones better. See? Let's say the red ones are mine and the blues ones are yours."

His finger pointing out the window. Me blowing air out of my cheeks.

"Have you ever been in love? Yes or no."

"My business."

"I think we should try it before we die."

"Huh?"

"Nothing. That's what I think."

I shivered. Did he already know that he would soon fall into a hole? If my mother knew about him then maybe he knew about her, about my father and the hole he'd fallen into forever, about the hole he himself would fall into. I had been holed up for three years, so what did I know about what other people knew of the world or the lives of others, about the things Chinese people know or what their ideograms know, with all those keys familiar with the universe?

Like in the *I Ching,* the *Book of Changes*, an ancient Chinese manual that teaches one to read the past, present, and future of an event simultaneously. You can do that by throwing three coins in the air or by picking yarrow stalks, either way you interpret the results according to horizontal lines that represent man or woman. It is the union of man and woman that reveals the present, past and future of things.

"I don't understand what you're saying."

"Forget about it, Jimmy. What do you know about the *Book of Changes*?"

"You're very smart, my brother's girlfriend. I can't wait to make love to you at the beach."

I took a marker from my backpack and wrote the Chinese character I invented on his wrist. The key to "water" plus the key to "equal." I wrote it three times, all up his arm, like the present plus the past plus the future, but he just kept looking out the window. Then he turned.

"How come you're writing those things?"

"No, it's nothing, Jimmy, it's just my ideogram."

"But I don't know how to read them, I've forgotten piles of Chinese characters."

"But this one doesn't exist, Jimmy. Let me teach you how to read it. You just have to say my name and my surname. Say

'Camelia Mega . . . ' By the way, what's your real name? Jimmy isn't a Chinese name."

"Jimmy is a really cool name."

"Fine, but what's your Chinese name?"

He saw Scarborough station in the distance and started clapping his hands. "Here we are," he cried, still clapping and fouling his face with big smiles. Key to "name": "darkness."

The sea was rough. We struggled against black waves, water coming in at every opening, in our noses, our mouths, and even our ears. I spat the water out, and the sea spat me out, pushing me back like an annoying thought.

Jimmy swam faster and pulled several yards ahead of me. "Jimmy!" I yelled but the "m"s just gurgled over my tongue and mixed with the seawater. My eyes were burning. I was terrified to look down; who knew what was down there. Then a wave swallowed me whole and I found myself, eyes wide open, in a spin dryer of fish in movement. There was that euphoric light on the rocks right below me. A web of light blue motes chased one another, consumed each other, exchanged their light like living cells, cells of a gigantic organism that was breathing me in and vomiting me out, growing, drowning me, with its bones of rock and its seaweed hair.

Finally, I reemerged and Jimmy was swimming towards me, "Oh god, I was really scared that you had drowned." His hair like brushstrokes on his large forehead.

We got to the inlet safe and sound and with us the seaweed-stuffed cadaver of a Heineken bottle. I leaned back into that prodigious universal judgment, over the animal energy of the waves castigating the sand and chewing on the reef, vomiting lascivious foam petticoats onto the too black rocks of the inlet.

My heart was beating hard.

Jimmy took me silently, and I was grateful to him.

Everything else was already yelling for us. The universe was the ventriloquist of our united bodies.

"Isn't it incredible being part of the world . . . ?"

"I don't understand you, Camelia. But you're beautiful."

"No, I'm not beautiful at all. You don't understand a bloody thing."

I had his semen on my leg. I was looking up at the rocks above us and I felt the liquid growing warmer, it was moving. I looked down and discovered it had turned red.

"What a pain, I've got my period."

"Doesn't matter, we've already made love."

"Right. Come on, let's go back to Leeds."

As usual, the train was on time. From my seat I saw the sky suddenly fall to pieces and become rain, enormous, corpulent, watery beasts dropping to earth. The sadistic wind rode them, hurling them against the glass, and the air got colder. And I saw everything, the gray light dribbling down from the sky onto the fields, onto the blue-stained sheep resounding with thunder. My head was spinning. I turned to Jimmy. He was peeling a peach with a knife.

"Let's go to the bathroom, Jimmy."

"I've already been."

"I know, but come with me, I said."

"I told you, I've already been."

"Fuck, get up, you idiot."

I knocked the peach down to the ground. Stupefied, he watched it as it rocked on the floor of the train. I knocked the knife down, too, and as it fell it traced a circle so perfect it made you want to cry. At that point he stood up and looked at me, strange.

I walked ahead of him, taking in the entire mass of seated passengers as I went, their fake books on Zen and the real ones they use to hold their train tickets, their hairless piglet-colored legs stretched out brazenly on the seats in front of them, and the children with their blue eyes scooting from one seat to another; one of them had a potato-shaped nose—"Now it's my turn!"—who knows what game they were playing, but that's the real game isn't it? Moving from one seat to another because the train is moving, and we're alive, all of us alive, and if you stop for a second you die. In fact, I kept on moving even though my belly and my kidneys were killing me, and every step provoked a warm flow between my legs.

I knew it couldn't last forever, it couldn't run down my legs all the way to my ankles, but the mere thought of something similar happening made the blood inch a little farther down my leg. I felt it trickling down my thighs, it filled the fold behind my knee, good god! it's on my foot!

"What, Camelia, what are you talking about?"

No, it wasn't blood, it was nail polish.

We barely fit in the bathroom, shoved against the wall, he and I, stuck between the toilet and the sink.

Me looking at the toilet and the sign that said: "Do not throw anything into the water closet." Him awkwardly removing my pants. He latched on to my breasts like the mollusks I used to try to pull off the rocks at Scarborough when I was a kid. But it was impossible, and my father would say, "You need a knife."

"For what?"

"No, nothing, Jimmy, nothing. Keep going."

"You seem strange."

"Quiet. I don't want to talk."

He pushed inside me and I could still hear the storm outside. I closed my eyes, Jimmy kept pushing, the blood kept flowing from that hole that can never be satisfied. Jimmy drew himself out of my flesh and he looked like a bloody newborn baby, umbilical cord still attached. He started crying when he saw the mixture of blood and sperm dripping from his member.

"What have we done, Camelia. Oh God!"

He sat down on the filthy floor tiles.

"Don't worry. It's impossible to get pregnant during your period."

"No, not that. I mean my brother, he's going to kill us."

"Your brother and I are not together, can't you get that into your head?"

"He thinks you are."

"What are you talking about, and why would you think that, did he say something?"

"No, but it's the same thing."

"What do you mean the, same thing? What's the same thing?"

"There was a girl, two yeas ago, and he used to say they were together."

"And so? What, Jimmy, for fuck's sake."

"We used to make love, like you and me. Wen found out and he said that Lily was his girl and that he was going to kill us both."

"And why did he change his mind?"

"No, he didn't."

"Jimmy."

"What is it?"

"Where's Lily now, where the fuck is she?"

The sound of the storm, of the train, of human beings talking, as if there wasn't enough noise already, that's what we are, noise upon noise.

I stared at him. We were intimate with the WC.

"What do you mean, Camelia?"

"What do you mean, what do I mean, are you a retard, I want to know if she's alive or not?"

"Of course she's alive."

"Goddamn it! You said that Wen wanted to kill her."

"Yes, he did, but then he took his anger out on me."

"How?"

"He forced me to stay shut inside the shop and he almost

never lets me go out. Never. You know the room with the red door?"

"But—"

"So I ruin the clothes," said Jimmy, giggling.

"So you're the one who makes them."

"No, they come from China, I ruin them, that's all. Then he throws them out. I used to pull them out of the dumpsters and put them back in the shop, so now he throws them out somewhere a long way from the shop, I don't know where."

"Holy god, you're a couple of lunatics."

I looked at him, his long back bent over the linoleum tiles of the bathroom, his legs folded uncomfortably, his narrow feet, the dismayed look on his face, his small nose, his mouth like an open, bloody noose. He struck me as someone I knew only from reading about him in a book, as if he had run away from some other story, one of those stories my father was always looking for, that are like pigeons, they're everywhere but you mustn't touch them because they're dirty. He looked like he'd just jumped from one of his dirty stories into my train carriage, into my bathroom smeared with blood, into my body, without even asking permission.

"Why are you looking at me like that, Camelia?"

"Are you sure that girl is still alive?"

"Sure."

"Then why did you say he was going to kill us?"

"Quit looking at me like that, you look crazy, you're scaring me."

"You're the fucking lunatic! You and your brother! Why would he think we're together if he rejected me? I wanted to make love to him and he didn't want to! I wanted him to be my boyfriend. I was in love, fucking hell . . . I only wanted to be happy! Instead, look at me, I'm in the bathroom of a train with an idiot! God, I should have known from the start not to get involved with a couple of lunatics like you! From the start!!"

Here's a riddle. The key to "start": "knife."

Jimmy was still crying. I was on my feet, stuck between the WC and the sink.

I felt sick and my stomach was swollen like a drum. I unbuttoned my pants again but they felt tight around my legs, too, and I could feel the blood stones melting in my stomach and releasing eddies of muck onto my thighs, so I took my pants off and finally saw the blood's face, with its limp body mowing down my leg hairs and stopping above my knee, two thick dark red lines like Satan's fingers.

I put my backpack on the ground and emptied it looking for a pad. Ten thousand ideograms drawn on yellow Post-its fell to the floor, among them the ideograms for "to fall," and the ones for "ten thousand" and "Chinese characters," and in the middle of all those characters a sheet of white paper, which I opened, and saw that it was, ah! the translation for Gagliardi Inc., or rather the last page of the translation for Gagliardi Inc., where were the others? And holy god when was it that I needed to deliver it?

It said: There are two possibilities at the end of the cycle:
Spin dry
No spin dry
I said: There are two possibilities for ending the cycle:
Suicide
Homicide
Anyway, there was no pad. I stuffed my panties full of tissues. "I think we're about to arrive in Leeds."

"I think it's three more stops," he said.

"I hate you, I want to die," I said.

When I got home I changed my clothes and collapsed on the bed. It was 6 PM and I was exhausted. My room was a terrible mess, T-shirts and socks everywhere, along with rebel ideograms that the wind had helped escape from the walls. Let's regroup. I have my Chinese lesson tomorrow and I still have to do my exercises, where did I put my notebook, and the translation, the other sheets, where are they . . .

With all that had happened I'd forgotten about my mother. Who knew if she'd eaten, if she'd washed, if she'd needed something when I wasn't there, who knew if she was still alive? I fell asleep fully clothed and slept for fifteen hours.

Inside my dreams, there was Jimmy's body, there were the waves pressed into my brain; I was afraid to wake up because they would come out my ears and crack my skull, and so I said, "Jimmy, keep pushing inside, I want to come again, I want to get some of this water out." But he said, "Look at it, it's red, your water is red," and I laughed, I cried, until I heard an obscene noise penetrate my dreams, a thumping sound, one after the other, and I yelled, "Oh god, Jimmy, it's Lily pushing on the cave, she's coming out of the stone, can't you hear it, her cadaver is getting closer, run!" But he smiled like a synthetic Buddha and said, "Don't be crazy like that, Lily is alive, I'm screwing Lily right now, it's fantastic, screwing until we die, oh oh," and I tried to wriggle free, and the thumping sound continued, the thumping on my front door, I woke up. Someone was knocking hard on our door.

"Who the fuck . . . "

I stood up confused, my head hurt, nobody ever came to visit us.

"Who is it?"

"It's Wen."

I opened the door. "Wen, what are you doing here?"

He was wearing an oversized black sweater and some fake Converses.

"Sorry, Camelia, I . . . I was worried about you."

"Why?"

"Because you didn't come to the lesson. You didn't answer your mobile. Did you forget that we had a lesson at nine today?"

"But isn't today Wednesday, March nineteenth, two thousand and eight?"

"No, Camelia, sorry but . . . today's Thursday."

"Thursday, March twentieth, two thousand and eight?"

Every time I exhausted all possible onomastic resources I felt a shiver similar to an orgasm.

"Yes, naturally."

"I overslept, that's all. I was really tired."

"Are you sick?"

"No, I mean, just a bit. My stomach. But it's normal."

"You're not going to ask me in?"

"No, what are you thinking, you can't."

"Why? I invited you to my house?"

"Yes, but my mother's here."

Only as I said it did I conclusively remember her. Every now and again the thought of her had protruded from my dreams like a crow craning its neck on the branch of a tree, but I didn't pay it any mind and kept on dreaming. And now, as I said the word "mother", her existence collided with me in all its tragedy. How could I have forgotten her? I ran into her room leaving Wen standing outside and the door half-open.

Livia was on her feet in front of the open window. I could hear Wen's footsteps inside the house. "Don't come in, Wen. I'm coming!"

My mother turned and started to smile, a slow fixed smile like on a plastic doll, maybe Chucky.

"How are you, Mamma?"

She opened her eyes wide and replied the look, *You have to tell him what you're doing with his brother now and that you're in love with him and you have to quit doing those disgusting things for the love of god.*

"Fuck off! Until recently you didn't give a shit whether what I was doing was disgusting or not, all you cared about was whether I was washing you and serving you, and they're not disgusting, it's what I want, and Wen is a bastard, can't you get that into your fucking head?"

You're a disappointment you're doing things that are immoral.

"You're immoral! You're a terrible mother! I've been your bloody servant for three years, for fuck's sake!"

You're heartless you ought to be ashamed and you talk like a fishwife.

"You're not the only one suffering, do you understand that or not?"

If you don't tell that poor boy I'm going to tell him what you do with his brother for god's sake is a scrap of honesty so difficult you don't even seem like my daughter.

"Shut up!"

I picked the key up off the floor.

You want him to kill you like he killed that girl that's it isn't it?

"What are you saying? Wen wouldn't hurt a fly! That girl Lily isn't dead! Jimmy's crazy, he talks a bunch of nonsense."

Ah so it's true that you want to get yourself killed. Why honey? Why do you want to kill yourself? I will not allow it. I'm going to tell him.

"Be quiet!"

I went out and locked the door. I could hear her banging on the door as I went down the stairs.

"Everything's ok. Wen, come into the kitchen, I'll get you some tea."

"What happened up there?"

"No, nothing, I was looking for something. Do you like raspberry tea?"

"Yes, of course."

He sat down, I threw out the dirty plates that were on the

table and turned on the electric kettle. He looked at the charred potholders and the blackened sponge in the sink, then he looked at the round coffee mug marks and the blobs of marmalade on the table. Then then then, he wouldn't stop looking, and each time he looked at something it became less dirty. His round clocklike face measured the arrested time in my house and, just by looking around, set it moving again.

"Were you arguing with your mother?"

"Yes."

I turned instinctively towards the stairs, towards her room, which couldn't be seen from there. She had stopped beating on the door.

"What are you looking at?"

"Nothing. Why are you sulking?"

"I'm not. It's my face, sorry. Listen, so you didn't come to the lesson today because you slept for an entire day?"

"God only knows. A whole day . . . No, not an entire day exactly, who do you think I am?"

"You said that."

"Yes, but then . . . I watched a movie too."

"What movie?"

"*The Hole.*"

"*The Hole . . .* "

"Yes, it's an American movie about some kids who lock themselves in a hole. Then their friend, the one who's supposed to let them out, never comes back and they all die."

"You know, the girl in the hole with them has the key all along."

"What are you talking about?"

"I swear. I've seen that movie."

"I've seen it, too. And if she had the key all along, it makes no sense at all. Why didn't she open it? Why did she let everyone die?"

"Because she liked the boy who was in the hole with her."

"Oh, so what? She could have been with him out of the hole, too."

"No, outside the hole he ignored her."

"Well, anyway, you're making all this up. I saw it and it's not like that."

"Did you watch it to the end?"

"Mm . . . no."

"At a certain point you discover that it's another thing entirely."

"Wen."

"Yes."

"There's something I want to talk to you about."

"What?"

The kettle was making a racket, it was the rain on the train windows, but also the waves coupling recklessly with the sand, and what was inside the body of the sea, the fish eating other fish, and the squares of light dancing on the rocks, dancing and never stopping, flowing, like the blood that I lugged with me wherever I went. The kettle turned itself off.

"So?"

"No, nothing. Nothing important."

"No sugar for me."

"Actually, you're the one who has to tell me something."

"Oh yeah, what?" A noise. I turned towards her room, but the noise was coming from the street.

"No, nothing. Nothing. Let's watch some TV."

I turned on Channel 4. There was a shampoo commercial playing. Blond right down to her toes, a woman swore to me with a smile so alive that it was worth a thousand promises on the souls of the dead, that my hair would stay cleaner longer.

After Wen left I unlocked my mother's door, took off her tracksuit, washed her, put on her pajamas. I counted on my fingers and deduced that Wen was the fourth houseguest we'd had since the day of the accident. That is, if we count the journalists as a single guest.

I suddenly felt the need to open the windows and let in a bit of air. But my mother looked daggers at me and so I shut them and left as she turned to face the wall, her dirty hair wound in a single oily braid. For the first time, I left her door agape, like an open sarcophagus.

I changed and went to bed. And at some point during the night, who knows what time it was, some anonymous and ignoble hour, it occurred to me that I hadn't made any dinner and maybe (I say maybe because I couldn't be sure) no lunch either. I let sleep slowly close my eyes.

I dragged myself onto my feet at six and cracked an egg in the frying pan, pulled out the orange juice, and while I was standing there listening to the oil sizzle I realized something: it wasn't so long ago that I had bought batteries for the clock. I went into my room and turned the clock around. There were no batteries in it. She had taken them out. She'd come into my room without my knowledge and taken them. What a shit.

I put in new batteries and went to her room. I slammed the door as I entered. She was sleeping on her back like a mummy, her thin arms didn't fill the sleeves of her pajamas, which remained half empty, crossed over her chest like finish line ribbons. She wasn't wearing the faded pajamas I'd dressed her in the night before, as I did every night, but her fancy white silk ones. Who knows when she'd exhumed them from the wardrobe and why she'd changed. I hung the clock on the wall on the empty nail. "Breakfast is ready. Get up."

She replied with a lazy smile that meant *SSSSSSSH,* with seven "S"s, and her eyes still closed, and the sweat tracing "O"s in the armpits of her pajama top. Yes, that's the only thing she likes to do: drown her clothes in all the liquids she's capable of.

The lessons continued, but so did the trips to Scarborough

every Wednesday. At lunchtime Jimmy and I would go for a walk on the main street. It smelled of fish. The sea followed us but at times it changed color. There were a bunch of casinos and every tobacco store sold porn magazines. The people went out walking, plump and happy, rubber flip-flops, the light revealing the morbid yellow of their hair and the swinish pink of their skin. We bought cheeseburgers and fries and went back to our cave.

We had sex. At least twice in a row. Occasionally three times. Nothing else mattered.

I wrote my personal ideogram on Jimmy's perfect chest and sometimes he laughed because it tickled. He planted his kisses of a hysterical child all over my body.

I watched the seagulls fly away and become the ideogram for "see," an open square with two curved lines sliding from it, I opened my legs and I, too, was that ideogram, and Jimmy wrote it inside me, filling me with his secret ink, and I said, "Let's do it again," but the sound of my words reached me on tiptoes, from behind the waves, behind the rain, ah! I hadn't even noticed the rain.

"I hadn't noticed either. Yeah, let's do it again, I really want to."

Then we'd go back to the shore like rebellious flotsam, our feet full of seaweed and sand. The sound of the ocean followed us, reminding me of that tubular African instrument that imitates the sound of the waves. In Scarborough it's the other way round, the waves imitate the sound of that instrument.

There were a boy and a girl, they were kissing in a strange way, like cats, and Björk was playing on the radio. Yes, it was really her. How long since I had heard her! I walked closer, the music grew larger, the high notes broke apart the incessant sound of the sea. "Look at the speed out there / It magnetizes me to it . . . "

I went home and nothing changed. Nothing changed even when

I went to lessons with Wen. The sound of mobiles and the beep of the oven and the alarm clock pushed their way into my daydreams, but I could only think of Scarborough. At home, on the street, at the supermarket, in shops. The moments with Jimmy's body stretched out like an elastic band; I undressed him continuously, and when I'd taken his clothes off, I peeled off his skin, too. His grid-like rib cage was the ideogram for "sex," the one with the key for "heart" on the left and the one for "life" on the right.

"Camelia, are you listening to me?"

"Yes, Wen."

When I got home at night I took a long shower. I stayed under the hot water until my fingertips became soggy paper. My mother watched me from the other side of the shower.

"What are you doing here? Wait your turn. No, you know what? I'm not washing you. Do it yourself."

And she reached into the pocket of her tracksuit. She slapped a photo against the glass of the shower. Through the steamy glass I could make out a tree with a thick crown, and around it, out of focus, a thick, luminous field

I got out of the shower. She stood there holding the photo up as if it were a trophy. The tree stretched toward the sky with so much sanity and passion. I could see it moving. The blurred lawn at its feet was an entire nation of adoring subjects on their bended knees offering human sacrifices.

She said the look, *Why do you sacrifice humans?*

I took the photo from her without even drying myself. It got wet. The tree was as near to the universe's vitality as anything could be. It was incredible that a few sixtieths of a second of light entering the lens, a precise aperture setting, a single choice about composition isolating one thing and leaving the rest behind forever, that these things together could create an image like that.

"Did you take this? Really? It's Hyde Park, isn't it?"

My mother had gone all the way to Hyde Park.

"Did you really leave the house?"

She smiled like a human being. God had to work for six days to create the cosmos in all its beauty. All my mother had to do was stop by Hyde Park.

It was like old times when she could just raise an arm and the whole world started playing. If she moved a finger the wind on the windows went *do-re-mi*. If she adjusted her hair a little, the fridge intoned a B-sharp. Her unwitting talent for being the conductor of universal beauty! My heart was pounding.

"Don't tell me that you actually went to the photography class?"

She smiled again.

"Why didn't you take me to the park with you?"

She took the picture back.

"Mamma, please, are you listening to me?"

She walked out of the bathroom.

My Chinese got better and better, which must be why April came.

Whatever happened now, whether it was homicide or a tsunami or a plague of locusts, I would know how to translate it into Chinese.

Thursday, April third, two thousand and eight, Wen, whose hair had grown longer, said, "I like flowers."

I said: "*Wo xihuan huar.*"

Him: "I'm happy today."

Me: "*Jintian wo hen gaoxing.*"

When I got home I found the wheelie bin full of my father's clothes: his Beatles T-shirts looked as if they'd been arranged according to the size of the holes in them. Then there were his black Nikes and his collared shirts. And on top, his notebook with its creased leather cover, the pages themselves impregnated with the leathery smell. The stories of an avid journalist, his stories, were still in there, masquerading as handwriting tending toward hieroglyphics. Stories of things that exist and maybe some that don't, stories that are now being eaten by worms.

I put them back in the garbage where they could commune with the putrid smell they deserved.

"You did the right thing by throwing everything out," I told my mother. She was sitting with her back to me in the kitchen dressed in her white and blue patterned silk Alexander McQueen, her hair was loose and clean and lay on her shoulders, a vigilant blond like a desert sun, almost white, flashing shadows and light.

"Mamma, what's going on?"

She lifted her Polaroid camera off her knees and pointed it at me. I opened my eyes wide.

And if you count to three, my love . . .

. . . You will get better? You'll be a person again? You'll talk again?

She lowered the lens to the floor, pointing it at a daisy that had mysteriously ended up in our kitchen.

The white light flared.

"Mamma, it's beautiful, why are you dressed up so nicely? Mamma, are you listening to me?"

She stood up and went to her room, her heels echoing through the whole house.

That's how we made it all the way to April ninth. Nobody expected as much on Christopher Road. Scarborough was crowded with happy English people expecting to go for a swim. I swam past them with Jimmy ahead of me on the way to our cave.

When we returned to Leeds he wanted to accompany me home, so I took him to Victoria Road, to my old apartment, the one I never lived in.

Everything on Victoria Road forces you to be happy, the goth-ic beauty of the spires, the elegance of the dark bricked row houses interrupted only by the evergreen-even-when-dead plants. On Victoria Road if you're not happy, you are prosecuted.

A young couple lived in the apartment now. They were far too blond and they smiled far too much. Excessive smiling had already given them deep wrinkles around their mouths, and still they went on smiling, each smile bringing another one right behind it—gateway smiles. Those smiles think they're Christ's emissaries, they think they must convey a noble imperative of well-being to all.

He was an architect and no, he said, my things were no longer there, and in fact he had no idea what I was talking about. Then they asked us if we wanted some tea. Jimmy nodded and I said that I would have decorated the apartment better than they had, red walls were maybe ok for bulls, at most, and what was that, a massage armchair.

"Excuse me, where's the bathroom?"

"Back there, don't you remember?"

"No, I never lived here."

"So, why are you looking for your things?" He smiled.

I went down the short corridor. Through an open door I caught a glance of a familiar face. Björk! That was my room and my poster was still there. They'd framed it, bastard thieves, and she looked like a sad Snow White inside her crystal coffin. You've got to let posters breathe, let them feel the vibrations of the air on their faces; the corners have to stretch out; they have to turn yellow like people, over time, with the wind's touch and the passing years. But look at that! What a shame!

The embalmed face stared out at me with trepidation in its eyes, white on its cheeks and on the feathers on its dress, black glimmering in its sharp eyes and in the abyss of its partly closed mouth. I had to do something, I had to free her . . . "You'll meet an army of me."

The architect, alarmed, raced in when he heard the crash of broken glass. I thrust the encyclopedia of design that I'd used at him and ran out with Björk under my arms. Jimmy watched me run out with his tea in his hands looking as if he'd just arrived from a planet not mine. He followed me out yelling, "How cool, my brother's girlfriend!"

We ran down the stairs like children, our arms in the air, breathing hard. The architect cursed us in German. Ah, I didn't know he was German. But nationality doesn't matter on Victoria Road, you just have to be happy. Jimmy, Björk, and I ran through the streets of Leeds laughing like lunatics.

When we got to the "Restaurant of Confucius" he wanted to go in at all costs. Then he insisted on dining in the private room, he said that's they way you do things in China. They took us to a room covered in black ideograms on beige parchment paper, with little black tea sets scattered between one character and another. The table could fit at least six people. It was round, black lacquered, a lazy Susan at the center for spinning the dishes.

"What's written on the walls, Jimmy?"

"It says, 'The aroma of tea.' Fried lily petals and glazed duck?"

"That's what I had last time. That's the only thing written on this whole wall?"

"But fried lily petals are delicious."

"I know, but I've already had them. Listen, Wen explained that each character has to be written within an ideal square but on this wall they all seem to be different sizes—"

"Do you want fried lily petals or not?"

"No, let's go somewhere else. This place makes me think ugly things."

"I'm going to order them for myself, the petals, you do what you want."

We ate an entire Peking duck, with all that onion and fennel you've got to put on it. When we'd finished my stomach hurt.

Jimmy, his lips smeared with sauce, was staring at me with that look of his, like the face of a gigantic child whose teacher knows he is dying to answer her question.

"Not here, Jimmy."

His long hands sought out my thighs under the table.

"I said not here!"

He slipped under the table and started eating my legs and my thighs and I could feel his slow tongue.

I put my finger in the red sauce on the table. I wrote my secret ideogram on the table.

Cameliamega on the marble.

Cameliamega on the empty stinking plate.

Jimmy came up from under the table and pulled me down onto the floor, he tore off my red shirt with the buttons that led to a banana shaped hole over my belly. The floor was tiled with little light blue tiles like the kind you find in a swimming pool.

During the wash cycle the porthole.

Jimmy got on top of me and entered me. His huge mouth smiling above my breasts, his longest-fingers-in-the-kingdom fingers squeezing them as if he were wringing out wet rags, his fingernails like huge mirrors.

"You're beautiful, my brother's girlfriend. I want you to be with me until we die."

"What? We're not going to die, Jimmy! We're not going to fucking die together!"

"We are. He's going to kill us both, I'm sure of it, but I want you anyway."

I tried to wriggle free but I was his prisoner. With his left hand he squeezed my right breast hard and with his right hand he held my left arm down. I felt pain collapsing into minuscule circles beneath my elbow. The smell of his sweat and his spicy breath assaulted my nostrils. And so did the strong smell of disgorged duck slowly cooked and soaked in a thick glaze that tastes of the candies you can pick out of baskets at Citibank while waiting in line with your mother. Especially when it's December twelfth, two thousand and four, and you have to leave her there standing alone because you have an appointment with the owner of an apartment at Thirty-two Victoria Road so he can give you the keys . . . *And if you count to three, my love, your father dies and I lose my mind! And if you keep counting you die too at the hands of the boy you love!*

There's only one thing missing, only one, my mother with her Polaroid camera. What's missing is a picture of this disgusting thing I've become.

Wait, we need one more picture. We need a photo that says "Before," and I am naked on the tiles with Jimmy on top of me, and another that says "After," and I'm dead as a doornail and Wen's hands are on the knife. Like in those ads for super diets.

"Yeees . . . You're so beautiful, forever, until we die, hold on, I'm coming . . . "

"Jimmy, isn't the character for 'Confucius' the same as the one for 'hole'?"

In and out and in.

And out.

He squirted his sperm into the ideal square of a light blue tile.

"It was fantastic, so fantastic, my brother's girlfriend. We're going to make love until he shoots us in the head and locks us in the red room forever."

I squirmed free of his heavy body and covered my ears. "Fuck you! Stop saying we're going to die."

The waitress came in, the one with the large bosom.

Isn't it true that the only thing lacking was my mother with the Polaroid camera? But all she does now is take photos of the universe's beauty. Now I no longer have the right to stop in front of her viewfinder.

Jimmy put his underpants back on as the Chinese woman chased us out in English. My tits to the wind, I picked up my crumpled and hot sauce stained Björk and apologized to the waitress—"Listen to me, for fuck's sake," I cried—but she was already calling the owner and wouldn't listen to me. Or maybe she didn't understand Italian.

When I got back to my neighborhood with my head spinning and the poster of my beloved favorite singer under my arm, I told the Pakistani guy that I would kill him if he didn't rent me a DVD of one of her concerts.

"Do you know who I mean? The Icelandic singer."

"Ah!"

He nodded and went over to the shelves.

He came back with the Icelandic movie in his hands, the one about the avalanche, the one where, when everyone dies, I can't stand it anymore to discover that I have survived.

At home I put the only Björk CD to have escaped the death of my father into my computer. It was covered in white out and superglue but it played all right, except for the fact that it made the sound of my mother playing *Casta Diva* on the flute.

I left my room shaken and there she was, at the top of the stairs, *la ti la so la do*, her hair hanging down to her shoulders, half consumed by the darkness, her flute tracing an elegant right angle against her body. She was dressed in red. She was playing the flute. The house became *ti la so so fa la so fa*.

I was shivering and I broke out in a cold sweat.

I don't know if it was because of *Casta Diva* or the blended sweater with more than a touch of acrylic.

I couldn't move. Small. Hers. She stood up there, so red at the top of the steep narrow stairs, stairs rotten with dust, like an upside-down Tower of Babel that instead of multiplying languages had destroyed them all. And all this, the elision of all languages, just to get to this moment, to her standing there mute and breathtaking as she always was after playing her favorite piece.

To me standing there, too, crying, looking up at her from the bottom of the stairs, like a living subtitle that reads: "The world has been waiting for you and lives yet for your beauty."

I remained at the foot of the stairs.

"Stay with us on Pearl Radio."

At some point Björk began as well—my computer is terribly slow. It was that song with the video where she goes into a museum and among the paintings there's a sleeping person on show. She puts a bomb next to the person and runs out of the museum. The bomb explodes and when she comes back everything is destroyed except the person sleeping. She has woken up and Björk hugs her.

Yes, there I stood, dazed, tears on my cheeks, the two melodies mixing like bodies.

"Mamma, come here, I want to hug you . . . "

She took her flute apart. She flicked the little drops of moisture out of the mouthpiece with a trio of deft gestures. She turned and went upstairs. She didn't hug me.

Back in my room I checked the dictionary. I was right, "Confucius" and "hole" are the same word, the word that shines in neon outside the restaurant. Its key is "child." I don't know if the restaurant is called Confucius or Hole. I stretched out on the bed.

The house had returned to silence.

I took the scissors from the table, opened the wardrobe. There was not a single dress left unscathed by my disfigurations. I stood on a chair to see if there were any left up top, but nothing doing, only sheets full of Chinese characters. I hadn't collected any clothes from the dumpsters for quite some time.

I sat on the bed. I looked at the scissors. I looked at my right hand holding the scissors. My right arm. Then my left arm where Jimmy had so violently held me down. I rested my arm on my bare thigh.

I pierced the inside of my elbow. The line formed the ideogram for "one," for a second, and then released the blood.

I kept going, first the two curved lines that cross one another and then the small one at the top. It was the character "Wen," but I'd completely messed up the order of the strokes: first the small one, then the horizontal line, then the two curved ones. How the fuck could I have messed it up. I dried my tears and wrote it again, correctly this time, a little farther down my arm. Each line survived intact for an infinitesimal moment, then a long broken line dribbled down my leg meeting other lines along the way. My body was held together by that trail of blood from my elbow to my thigh. I recalled the Chinese legend that says that when a boy and a girl are destined for one another they are tied together forever by a red thread.

The next day was Thursday but it didn't matter because I was never going to lessons again. At ten past ten the telephone rang and kept ringing until it was swallowed by silence.

I turned on the TV, there was a costume drama. The women promenaded, their waists strangled by enormous skirts. I jotted down the keys I saw on my left leg. With the scissors, I mean.

"Mother." "Child." "Door." "Wood." "King." Moon." The sound of rain falling on the street outside was louder than the TV. Like a dubbed dialogue slightly out of sync. Like a chorus of lying voices telling you the wrong story; certainly not my story, it certainly wasn't me taking nicks out of my legs while outside the evil spring advanced in Yorkshire installments.

The blond woman in the film spoke rain and her mother, as she drew nearer, replied in rain. I lowered the volume, *plic plic plic* went the rain, *plic* went the hooves of the horses pulling the carriage in the movie.

Outside, the endless sadomasochism of earth and sky, clouds lacerating innocent lawns with water; and there I was behind closed windows, still a participant in the cold vicious eclipse of day, in the coming of night, which dropped like a corpse thrown from above.

The bastard Leeds night started falling before lunch. It was incapable of waiting its turn. In fact, the only place in Leeds you ever see daylight is on TV. It's a tall tale, a myth, like when they thought that in America the fruit was giant size.

In honor of the rain I described the key "water" with three quick incisions below my kneecap. More blood going *plic plic*. In the movie, more mute words the meaning of which was *plic plic plic*. The final credits started rolling and I stanched the bleeding with a sheet I tore off the wall, the one with the ideogram for "poem" on it. And if you substitute the key for "poem" with the one for "person" the ideogram becomes "samurai."

While thinking, "Leeds is certainly not the most refined metaphor for death," I fell asleep.

Or perhaps I passed out. I don't know exactly which. I was out until the *plic plic* became a *ring ring*.

"Y . . . yes?"

"It's Jimmy. We have to go to Scarborough, now."

"What?"

"Let's go, I have to talk to you."

"It's raining, Jimmy."

"No, not anymore. The sun's out."

"What time is it?"

"One-fifteen."

"I'm not well and anyway I don't want to see anyone anymore."

"Why?"

"And if anything I'm supposed to go to lessons with Wen today."

"I'll come over to your place."

"I have to talk to you, too."

"What about?"

"I'm hanging up, my legs hurt."

"Why?"

"We have to talk, stupid. And you have to tell me the truth."

"Let's meet at the station."

I hung up. I threw the scissors hard at the television.

They hit a woman in blue on a show that had just come on. I realized that until a few episodes back she'd been full of wrinkles. The scissors slid down towards the rug.

They left a crack like a signature with which the world ratified my death. It was completely stylized, as fashion dictates. I stuck my finger in it and discovered that it was deeper than I thought right where the scissors had struck; it was a kind of crater. When I pushed on it the colors of the movie became one of those warped rainbows you find on the sidewalk, one of those miracles of meteorological mockery where you're walking down Christopher Road after the rain in search of a dumpster that is not completely overflowing and suddenly beneath your feet you find all the colors of the cosmos.

All that waste of spontaneous chemical reaction when they could simply send me an armed kid to say, "Your money or your life ha ha I'm joking who would want your fucked up life."

I got up. The husband of the woman in blue had just died. Undoubtedly because the actress's facelift had used up the budget for the entire cast.

I washed. I dressed.

Outside it was so decidedly April that I had to shield my eyes with my hand, too much light, so much that you couldn't believe God only took a day to make it. I walked slowly, squeezing myself into what shade there was.

I boarded the train and sat next to him, to the boy who made everything worse. He was eating a banana and reading a Korean manga and I said, "Listen," but he was laughing at the comic book and his wide-open mouth was stuffed with pulped banana.

His laughter was different, almost cruel.

Outside the rain-soaked fields rocked hypnotically under the hooves of the grazing sheep and horses. You couldn't tell where they stopped rocking, where the grass ended and death began.

The rain humiliated the grass for almost forty-six minutes and then we arrived. In the cave I pulled Lily from my thoughts like a malignant tumor and put her between Jimmy and me, smack in the middle, right where the hole was. Jimmy said, "Lily what?" as he undid the ties at the back of my bikini.

"Is she dead or not? Fuck! Leave my costume alone."

"No, jeez, she's not dead."

"What's her surname?"

"This is like in the movies when the police interrogate you."

He jumped on me without even looking me in the face. He was wearing a red costume with the words "Fruity dance 2night" on them, followed by some Chinese characters.

"Wait, what are you doing? Listen to me. Can you tell me why Wen thinks we're going together?"

He pulled my costume aside and entered me.

"Jimmy, listen to me for fuck's sake, explain it to me."

"Behave, my brother's girlfriend."

"Get out of me, you're really hurting me."

I couldn't get free of him. He held my wounded legs tight, he opened them like he wanted to pull them off my body. "Leave my legs alone, fuck, you're hurting me."

There was the fucking sea, in front of me, in spite of everything.

The sky was the exact same color that I used to draw it in preschool.

"I'm . . . coming . . . Let me come inside you my brother's . . . ahhh . . . you're beaut . . . "

"No!"

A warm spurt. He exited my body and stretched out belly

down on the hard rock. His remains on my burning thighs and inside me. Do not allow Chinese children with large mouths near the porthole.

"I met another girl."

"What, sorry?"

"You're not kind to me."

"But—"

"We're not going to see each other again, I don't want to."

"Who the fuck is this other girl?"

"She's from Shanghai. I met her on chat."

"Fuck you!"

I stood up quickly and turned away from him.

"Oh God, sorry, what have I done? Did I do that to your legs?"

"No, don't worry about it."

I fell into the water, the sudden cold shattered the pall of hot pain in my throat into a thousand pieces.

He stood up. "Where are you going, Camelia?" His voice was exhausted.

I looked at him and I almost felt pity. He stood there, his stump swinging between his legs, his astonished eyes like those in the head of a fish.

As he watched me swim away from him, he wiped away the semen on his thigh, and I washed the tears from my cheeks. He was saying things I could no longer hear. The sea became rough. The ideogram for "sperm" is the same as that for "purified." Also for "perfect." And "spirit" too. But also "demon."

The sun's warmth on my shoulders. I swam away, my eyes still on him. His extra-large mouth as he spoke those things I couldn't hear sliced into his cheeks.

"Why are you smiling, you piece of shit, when you just raped me then dumped me?"

"Whaaat?"

"Why are you smiling?"

A wave pushed me under and then spat me back up. I felt water in my nose and my head was throbbing. A hurtful red sky beseeched the night like a bloodied samurai imploring the final blow that will sever his head.

He was talking again and smiling, so tall and naked and wet standing in the middle of that grotto. All that, the sperm and his very smiley smile that spread from one cheeky cheek to the other, and his body so bodily as he watched me with his very feetish feet at the edge of the cave that slowly drew further and further away; all that effort at life, obtuse and treacherous life that goes by the name of Jimmy; all that effort when I could simply have tied a stone to my chest before jumping into the water.

What did it matter? Nobody will ever tell me that I'll always have a place in their heart. Instead, they'll find a place for me among the thorns and broken beer bottles in the deconsecrated cemetery.

I took the street from the station to the center of town under a stupid rain that fell and stopped, and then fell again, and then went away altogether.

Christopher Road was hot and wet like a whore. My eyes rained too, not to mention the sores on my legs. When I got home I had a headache. I had no idea where my mother was, and I stretched out on the bed.

I slept like my father, beneath tons of earth.

My mobile phone was vibrating under the blanket and I was suddenly awake. I answered without thinking. "Hello?"

"Good evening, Gagliardi Inc. here."

"Yes, I know, the translations . . . I know, I know, I haven't sent you the last one. You're firing me, I suppose, but it doesn't matter, I don't care."

"No, no, we're more interested in promoting you. Listen, we've organized a conference and the interpreter has a clash, if you could help me—"

"You mean translate into English what you and your colleagues say in Italian?"

"Yes, yes, are you available?"

"No."

"We're so grateful. We'll be expecting you on the eleventh at four."

"What did you say?"

"Excuse me?"

"When, exactly?"

"Tomorrow. We'll be expecting you, then."

"No, I'm not going to be there . . . Hello?"

He'd hung up. The sun tormented things with a light that fell lower and lower. A swift sunset ejaculated behind uniform roofs, then nothing, the open mouth of night, its slow rotting of the city, its tongue flicking identical silences over the houses of Christopher Road.

The elegant sound of high heels behind me.

I turned and saw my mother in her silk ice-colored Bernhard Willhelm dress, black bows fluttering down from the puffy sleeves to the embroidered lilies of the bubble skirt. I was just about to say how beautiful she was but she extended her arm and, smiling, handed me a flier. It was for an exhibition of photos by students in her class. Really, Mamma?

"And what day—"

She interrupted me with another smile.

"Mamma, what day is the show?"

She pointed to a line on the flier, and I read: "April 4 to April 7 at Joyce Hall."

She smiled. Not one of her typical smiles, the *Rest in peace* kind, but one of those that say, *All you need is love.* God, how different she was. She was different in her silence. Now it was a silence that was alert, hungry for my words; she devoured my sentences even before I let them out into the world.

She snatched them from my tongue.

"Mamma, I . . . "

They were hers before they were mine.

"Wait, Mamma, but . . . today is the tenth, the show ends tomorrow, why are you telling me now? Don't you care whether I go or not?"

Another smile.

"What are you smiling at? I enrolled you in that class, I was the one who convinced you to get off the fucking couch, all these years I'm the one who . . . "

She left, closing the door behind her. I fell back into the chair. Tears nosedived onto my cheeks like kamikaze pilots.

Night fell twenty minutes later. Stretched out on my bed I could hear the night owls, but it turned out to be my mother making noises as she slept even though it was only seven at night, and even though she was now a person who exhibited her photographs.

The pain in my legs masked all other pain. Livia whimpered again as she turned in her bed. I went up to her room, worried she might be having a nightmare. It could be one of those awful dreams, one of those where I have to hold her so tight she can hardly breathe, then she falls asleep on my shoulder.

I opened the door.

An ocean of clothes covered the floor. Radiant silks. Angora wool. Elegant pinstriped suits. The French dress with the embroidered cat, the slacks on sale with flower pockets, the linen top with the owl, the peach one with the Russian collar, the polka-dot jacket that my grandmother gave her after Livia's performance at the wedding of two Romanians . . .

She was standing on the bed, dressed in her frilly light blue Vivian Westwood with the sequins, matching nail polish on her toenails. She moved with agility and joy as she flipped through the folded silk scarves on the shelves above her bed. I had convinced her to buy that dress one day when we were in London.

In my language and in the language from which we stole the word, one says, "sequin." In my mother's language there is a specific gaze for venerating those bright disks right as you are bringing the flute to your lips on stage at a wedding. There's another one for grieving over them when you're too depressed and emaciated to wear them.

She chose a white scarf with light blue butterflies on it, and held it against her cheek and with her eyes said, *How do I look?*

I replied with the gaze, *You look fantastic. Where are you going?* but she didn't turn around to look at it. My face was dirty with tears. The faucet that had been sealed for years was now obscenely, uncontrollably open.

She dropped the scarf on the bed and returned her attention to the others. I stared at her thin white feet jumping on the sheets.

The bedsprings creaked.

"Mamma, listen to me, please. I'm talking to you."

There's no two ways about it: the creaking of bedsprings is identical to the sound of coupling turtles, when, even if you try to separate them with the broom, they continue without even noticing your presence.

I ran downstairs.

I woke my computer from its eight-day slumber.

And I searched for "Lily dead Leeds."

Ten thousand sites dedicated to floral funereal compositions!

The search engine asked if I was looking for photos.

I clicked on yes.

A profusion of brightly colored lilies of all sizes blossoming one after the other, bursting forth hysterically on my innocent screen. My eyes hurt.

Maybe there was something on her university's Web site! I wrote "Lily Leeds student of Chinese."

I got a link to restaurant in Peking that served only penises.

The journalist said that their specialty was a sauce made from deer penis.

I had to talk to Wen. I started writing him an email, choosing my words calmly.

At that point I had to confess everything.

I wrote:

"Dear Wen, (When I'm with you I feel awful and I can't find the right words in English or in Chinese, so I'm writing you a letter.)"

Then I told him everything, from the first day I had sex with his brother right up to now, to when Jimmy dumped me, and the tears were falling one after the other, and I asked him about Lily; I said I knew nothing about that story, but I did know that I wanted to be with him forever, no matter the price, and if he had told me that he killed his girlfriends in the end like Bluebeard, then okay, it wouldn't have mattered, if that were the price, okay, if I could only love his body once then even dying would be okay, I would carry that memory with me to the grave, a real memory, a happy memory, one was enough, just one amidst all the others that I didn't want in my head. "But, tell me, what happened to Lily?" I said.

I was shocked at the abject sugariness of what I had written but all in all it was fine the way it was. In movies sentimental bulimia worked like a dream.

When I looked up at the screen I was horrified.

Almost all the words had been transformed into cheeky yellow goggle-eyed faces, with demented grins and big hands applauding.

I tried to correct the letter but when I typed an apostrophe it become a tear. The colon became eyes, the "O"s were all mouths, and the dashes noses. An epidemic of half-witted smiles and cartoonish grins.

I deleted everything. The emoticons were slaughtered one by one together with the remains of my pathetic declaration of love. I started again. "Dear Wen" followed by a comma and the parenthetical. Fuck! "I have to confess something: I've been screwing that idiot of your brother for the past three months," I wrote. That's all.

A face sticking its tongue out had popped up between "something" and "'ve."

I closed my laptop furiously. I heard a crack that was even more despairing than usual and when I reopened it I discovered that two keys, Q and K, had died an awful death.

Their plastic remains lay there, detached, on the keyboard. I picked up the Q. Beneath the letter like a final testament addressed to me there was a mini porthole. In the porthole there was a little rubber volcano. I lifted it up with my fingernails. There was the naked porthole, a small metal disk in its midst.

I pushed it to see if it still worked.

Yes.

So those friendly letters are no more than useless masks, a concession to people who cannot bring themselves to face the porthole head-on.

I picked up the K next. The other keys were more difficult to extricate. I used my fingernails, then a hammer. The Delete key—that one really had no desire to be done away with. I had to hammer away at it three times.

The most willing martyrs were the squadron of numbered Fs on the top row. All I needed for the first six was a single blow, for the seventh I used my fingernails, and Failure8 and Failure9 followed 7 to the grave with honor.

My greatest conquest, however, was the tyrannical bloody shackle, the Shift Lock key, which is like the magic elixir that transforms Alice in Wonderland into a giant. It is the most democratic key, utterly unlike the Shift key, which only transforms single letters.

Fine! Away with him, too, and rest in peace. I typed "peace." Then I skinned all five letters.

After an hour, the keyboard was a necropolis of letters. Gone were the lunatic arrows and blustering asterisks, gone were the alphabetic ingredients for forming words that only formed emoticons anyway.

I felt honest. I closed my laptop and turned off my mobile phone.

Noise of Livia coming down the stairs in high heels. I stood. Her back was to me, her hair was tied into an impeccable bun, and her skin emitted a violent perfume. I took her by the shoulders and said with my voice, "You look beautiful, where are you going?"

She turned. Her long eyelashes, even without recourse to the banal ruse of eyeliner, were shameless. Her cheeks were the color red, and to hell with foundation. Her lips were the most beautiful and most natural shade of magenta I had ever seen. Light became color for no other reason than to express itself on my mother's body.

"You look so great . . . Won't you tell me where you're going?"

She spoke the gaze, *You'll be happy for me.*

And I replied the smile, *Why?*, which is actually one of the most difficult phonemes in the language of smiles, because you have to introduce surprise into the smile without undermining its fundamental joyfulness.

Livia was about to tell me a look when the doorbell rang.

Good god! It must be Wen, I thought. He'd read my email. But no, in the end I hadn't sent it. Then he must be here because I didn't go to my lesson.

Help! My heart was beating painfully everywhere. He mustn't see me in that state.

I stood up as my mother went to open the door, rocking side to side in her blue heels.

I washed my face and teeth twice, I brushed my hair. I rummaged in the dirty clothes-basket in search of a nice dress. There was nothing but an army of disfigured clothes.

I ran up to my mother's room, I tripped on the French dress, and chose a white suit that smelled of mothballs and nailed every winter you'd witnessed from the cheap seats of your crappy home on Christopher Road into your head.

I descended the stairs cautiously in my mother's shoes, which were two sizes too big for me, and in slacks that were longer than my legs and had collected half a kilo of dust by the time I got halfway down the stairs.

I uttered a dyslexic "Here I am" that even I didn't hear.

I raised my eyes from the shoes.

At the door there was a smile being worn by an extremely handsome man who was not Wen.

In this flaccid world, there's nothing unusual about someone showing up on your doorstep who will never save your life. I stood there, my enormous heels of white varnish glued to the steps as if, in the end, this story gone wrong was not really mine.

She said a smile called *Come on, come down*, and the translator's note read: "You're not going to believe this."

I descended the last few steps.

The marvelous stranger stood there in our doorway wearing a smile that could easily attain world peace. Thirty-two teeth thirty-two times perfect, wavy dark blond hair the color of a beach on a tourist brochure, a thin nose, and blue XL eyes. His long hands were buried in the pockets of his pinstriped trousers, which were of a honeymoon-on-a-yacht color, a moonless midnight blue; and he wore an ice-colored shirt reminiscent of the iceberg that sinks the yacht and provokes the newlyweds' tragic but terribly romantic death.

And there she was, staring at him, all aglow, Livia Mega, my mother. I will never believe it.

"Hi Camelia, I'm Francis, your mum's photography teacher. You know, she's really good."

" . . . "

"I'm going to steal her from you for a couple of hours, ok, we're going for some Chinese."

"At the restaurant where they quarter the duck in front of you?"

"What's that, sorry?"

"Nothing."

As my mother pulled on her light blue raincoat, Francis, all excited like, told me that he, too, was a widower. He wouldn't stop smiling. He said, "Your mother and I, you know, we have the same pain in our hearts."

How sweet! What is it they say? "Two hearts beating beneath one gravestone." And another thing: anyone over the age of eleven who uses the word "heart" should be sent straight to a psych ward.

"She was in coma, my wife. I didn't leave her side."

My mother sporting a smile called *compassion*.

Me with my fists clenched and the wounds on my legs throbbing.

Him banging on: "All those tubes attached to her body, poor thing." And between one word and the next he flashed a subliminal smile that advertised the joy of new love.

And still more: "At night we'd pray together until she fell asleep."

Please roll the closing credits!

Not a chance. Francis continued with his discount store melodrama. "Life can be cruel to the kindest, the best of people." And: "When she died I didn't say a word for a week."

The things one says to impress a mute blonde!

"You know, she was in coma for a whole year, Camelia, and it took a year after that for my son . . . "

No, a son too, no, enough is enough. How could my mother have chosen a man like him? I was paralyzed by anger, and there I stood before that man who had showed up out of nowhere, that man handsome enough to be sued, that man who continued to smile at me until the bloody end.

"Mamma, don't go."

"Come on, Camelia, give your mum a bit of freedom."

"What did you say?"

My mother smiled *Let's go*. They walked out of the house together and sat in the car, one of those Japanese cars, shiny and sleek, fire red, without a single dent or scratch. The headlights already on.

She put her seatbelt on. I walked closer. He said: "Camelia, can you take a photo of us?" He handed me his mobile phone through the window.

I aimed it at the happy couple. I took a few steps back so I could get everything in the picture including the view of a wheelie bin through the car window. They were smiling. It was a reference to a movie that was a remake of a movie that was the remake of another movie that was based on a book based on a true story.

I said: "One . . . "

My mother in a car with that marvelous man who had come from nowhere.

"Two . . . "

My mother in a car with my father and me as we head for the airport. "Papa, am I going to like England?"

"Three . . . "

My father in a car with Liz Turpey saying something like: "Do you like the way I do it?"

" . . . Cheese!"

Francis said: "I think you took it the wrong way around."

I looked down. What an idiot! The photo showed a pocket of the suit I was wearing. "When are you coming back, Mamma?" I cried.

The car sped off.

Everything hurt.

After a terrible three-minutes-more-or-less I started walking. I hadn't closed the door and I was freezing to death.

I walked and walked and the wall appeared, the wall that separated people like me from all those different and very beautiful houses, from their dark brown brick streaked with nostalgic moss, from their bright blue doors and white gates with heart-shaped arabesques, from their black iron fences, from the complexity of branches that sketched convulsed ideograms on the sky. Like a muzzle over a scenario that is so beautiful it hurts, the Headingley wall is the Great Wall of Leeds; it protects me from life, and protects life from me.

Behind the wall, among the houses, a profusion of gigantic rare plants, leaves as broad as boats, branches as robust as light poles, veins as marked as electric wires. Good god, they are capable of photosynthesis even in the absence of sunlight, insects pay to repose on them, and, naturally, they cure all ills, even death.

I clenched my fists tight, digging my fingernails into my flesh, my head was ready to explode, and I kept walking. The tallest tips of the plants, so boldly bright and sleek, were excessively green, the kind of green you see in Japanese cartoons when the heroines change form, or the kind of green on that iridescent paper they use for snacks. The kind of green, that is, associated with happy fucking babies.

They moved in a magic breeze that, on my face, became a slap. It sent my hair over my nose, it troubled my eyes, and I was dying of cold. I kept walking but I was shaking all over and beneath my suit the ideograms on my legs sent flashes of pain through me. The florist was closed, but not closed like the newsstand, closed like a grave. Closed in a way that made throwing up the shutters inadequate and useless, it would take a deal with the devil at the very least.

I passed the cemetery and came to Wen's shop. It was closed

too. I sat down outside. The blood-colored sign read "Shouxue Shangdian." At the third lesson, Wen had told me that "shang-dian" means shop and "Shouxue" was his mother's name.

Now I know that "shouxue" can also mean "defend the snow."

Also, now that I think about it, "hole."

I searched my jacket for my mobile. All I found was the little knife.

I pulled it out of my pocket and right below my knee I wrote the ideogram for "death" above the ideogram for "death." Like when you write "I will love you forever" on a gravestone.

The key for "night" to the right, that sort of "T" to the left. And the roof for protection on top. "Night" quivered for an instant and began to bleed. Night fell. It was cold and it hurt.

My disfigured legs carried me to the cemetery. I climbed over the gate and sat with my back against the first gravestone I found.

I closed my eyes but the darkness was the same.

I awoke with my head resting on a premature death. The grave of a twelve-year-old had made my forehead ache, thanks largely to a little kneeling angel with his three feet of wing draped over the plinth.

I raised my eyes to a dawn that only those well trained in the ante-meridiemal timidity of Leeds would recognize as such. On the other side of the cemetery steeple a mini sun expressed itself in blurry red, like one of those holes my mother photographed.

My mother!

In my head, the word "mother" snapped open like a folding chair and became "my mother's new man."

I stood up. The day lurked around on a nocturnal background. In Leeds, daytime is merely a point of view.

Weeds taller than me enchained the emptiness, masking the gravestones. I climbed over the gate.

A crow spoke on my behalf, as I had no desire to speak myself. In my mother tongue you say, "*Neanch'io voglio vivere*," "I don't want to live either." In my mother's tongue it is a gaze that buries itself in the weft of the carpet and then lifts to meet my own. I mean, it *was* that, before her gazes turned toward that man, without warning, without so much as a will, and I was left with slimy sidelong glances, nothing more.

Wen's shop was open.

Everything that is capable of producing pain in a human body hurt. I was cold all the way to my memory. All my reminiscences had blue lips.

I approached slowly and waited for Wen to see me. My heart faster than the speed of light. When he ran to open the door for me, I said: "Don't you like me at all?" and my voice emerged in many different tonalities, one following the other, like old cassettes when the batteries in your player are running down.

Wen held my fingertips lightly. "I like you so much."

"Then why? Why don't you want me?"

"There's a reason."

"For god's sake, what is it?"

He started to sob faintly, right there in the doorway, his head hung down, his ink-stained mini fingers pressed over his eyes.

"Talk, you bastard!"

"No."

The red cat sang like a drunkard.

"No? Well, I have the courage to talk to you, I do. Are you listening? I fucked your brother. Happy now? Lots of times, in Scarborough, and I liked it a lot!"

He started to shake, like in a movie. His eyes were those of a petrified rabbit. I put my hand on his shoulder because I was afraid he might fall, or, I don't know, that he might break, he looked more fragile than I had ever seen him, almost as if he might disappear at any moment. The minute my fingers reached him he started sobbing louder, he held me, he pressed his head against my shoulder. And I too imprisoned his body in my arms.

I said: "*Wen wo ai ni.*"

The pressure of his head against my shoulder.

Of his mind on my body.

Of his existence on mine.

Finally.

He said, "No, you don't love me, it's not true, you're a liar, you went with my brother and I knew I knew I knew."

He ripped his arms from my back.

"I knew," he said again, translating the words simultaneously into infantile sobs. The red cat honked. Wen went back into the shop. Then he turned and looked at my face, which, in my mother's tongue, was pleading itself hoarse.

My face that in my mother tongue, however, was only crying.

My horrible face that deserved to die.

"Wen, is Lily dead?"

I went in and closed the door behind me.

"Sorry, Camelia. I can't be with you. I don't want to hurt you."

"But I—"

"Go back to Jimmy, you'll be happy together. Bye."

He opened the red door, went through it, and closed it behind himself. On my feet to the right of the cash register, I had forgotten how to breathe.

On Briggate in a smelly takeaway I ate two plates of fish & chips, which I detest. As I filled my stomach the tears dried on my cheeks and my heartbeat slowed. I paid. Fuck, I couldn't afford not to go to the conference now. My money was running out.

It was still early. I ambled on witless leaden legs. On a side street, squatting down between a shoe shop and another takeaway, was the "Tattoos for All" parlor. Standing at the top of the street I felt a hot flush in my legs.

I walked towards the shop. In the window there was one of those posters showing pictures of former customers, a mosaic of arms and backs and shoulders and chests all without their accompanying bodies, all sporting twisted dragons or stupid tribal motifs, or the names of people, or horrendous goblins that looked like me. And there were legs in bloom, and cartoonish butt cheeks, and a daring dolphin on somebody's back. Every one marginalized by the body to which it belonged, slapped down on a poster next to a price, like in some zombie-world McDonald's. I stood dazed before those morsels of human flesh alone in the world, my body frozen stiff and death in Chinese pulsing on my leg. I felt like one of them.

A boy with green hair came out of the shop. "Can I help you?"

I went in.

"I want you to write this?"

"Sorrrrrryyy?" he replied. Too many "r"s, I thought, he must be Scottish.

I took a pen from my bag and wrote my personal ideogram on my hand. Right where I had once written that I had to wash my mother and before that that I wanted to withdraw from university.

The boy said, "All rrrrrright", and pointed to the bed. On his right arm a bright blue stream, two pale green houses in the distance and a seagull in the sky.

I sat down. Body parts were hanging wherever you looked. Near the cash register a religious thigh: a Hail Mary hid cellulite that stretched down to the knee. Then two hands joined together with tattooed rings. Then a muscular arm with some writing in Arabic. And to my right, framed in pink, a pair of poetic glutes signed William Blake. The poem began on the left butt cheek and ran top to bottom like in Japanese, ending with the "y" of "symmetry," which stretched spiralform down toward the anus.

"Wherrrrrre?"

I hadn't even thought about where to put it. Others mustn't see it. I exposed my breast and pointed to my heart. "Here."

"Herrrrrrre?" he said.

I nodded and laid back. He told me to take off my bra. I threw that trifling thing of threadbare black cotton over towards the trash-can.

He drew the outline of the tattoo. Then he spread a color-less cream over my chest, and unsheathed a needle. I closed my eyes, but the body parts slipped in behind my eyelids.

Only it was all different. I was the parts of the dismembered body. The hand was mine, the arm mine, the butt cheeks mine. The ankles mine. The back mine. I saw everything with monstrous clarity. Small garments made of human flesh. And the river of Knaresborough carrying them all away.

The young man began. I felt the pressure and then the slow incision, cutting into me as one day someone would carve my gravestone. What a disappointment: it hurt less than all the rest.

First there was water.

Then there was the solid edifice, like a prison, inside of which appeared the line and the square.

He inflicted one stroke after another. Sometimes I opened my eyes and spied his green hair, green like the forbidden plants behind Headingley Wall.

My body saying blood. My leg and my brain saying death. And my mother who, if she'd been there, would have taken a photo of my navel. No, I was forgetting that she had been cured of the holes, she had found a man, and she no longer wanted me.

I opened my eyes. The tattooist's head smiled, his hand pulled the needle away from my heart, and he dabbed my chest with a cotton swab. First he asked me in vain if I wanted to see it, then he stuck a transparent wrap over the ideogram and said that I had to avoid alcohol for three days. He picked my bra up off the floor and threw it to me with an expression that said, "As if there were something to fill it."

His legs went towards the cash register. His left hand full of cheap glittering rings handed me a slip of paper with the name of a cream I had to buy.

"One hundrrrred pounds please."

All those wasted "r"s, when he could simply have pushed the needle through to the pulmonary artery.

The headquarters of the washing machine company was large and modern with a gigantic green-red-and-white-striped sign on a gray pollution-stained wall. I went in and approached the reception desk but then said, "Who gives a shit, I'm leaving."

The fat guy came out of nowhere and grabbed me by the shoulder forcing me to go with him into the other room. Unwitting couples that had been told over the telephone they'd won something were sitting in the first four rows.

The fat man took the stage with me and said, "*Non esagero se vi dico che le nostre lavatrici sono le migliori.*"

And me: "I'm not exaggerating when I say that our washing machines are the best."

Him: "*La nostra tecnologia Macchia-stop elimina le macchie piu' difficili.*"

Me: "Our Stain-stop technology eliminates even the toughest stains."

He was a prefect reproduction of the management apparatus. I swallowed his Italian words and regurgitated them in the soft smoothed sounds of English.

He said: "*Adesso vi mostro il risultato di un lavaggio standard.*"

I said: "I'm now going to show you the results of a standard wash cycle."

The fat man went back to the fake washing machine behind him.

He opened the porthole.

He pulled out a white shirt and a pair of white trousers.

In the room, bored chatter.

He said: "*Bianco come la neve!*"

I said: "White as snow."

He said: "*Bianco come latte, signore and signori!*"

I said: "White as milk, ladies and gentlemen."

He said: "*Un perfetto bianco per una vita perfetta.*"

I said: "Yes, your life is perfect, while mine is only good for picking up the shit your dogs leave on the street."

He said: "*Per una dimostrazione gratuita, chiamate il numero verde zero sette uno tre nove.*"

"Shit, didn't you hear what I said?"

He slapped me on the arm. "Quiet, kid, what's the matter? Just keep translating."

"What do you mean, what's the matter? I'll tell you, I'm going to kill myself in front of all these people, then let's fucking see if you realize I exist."

The fat man frowned. From the audience a ripe voice said, "Excuse me, I have a question about the Stain-stop technology."

I pulled the little knife out of my pocket and pointed it at my heart. An old crinkled woman frittered away her last thread of voice to cry out. Other shouts followed. "What's she doing? Help!" They cried like chickens, and some made straight for the emergency exit. The alarm went berserk and the noise, apparently, provoked everyone to make more noise, because they started roistering in every imaginable dialect of Great Britain. Thrown into confusion by the bleating alarm they went off on a boisterous game of goose in search of a door they were authorized to pass through.

The fat man swore in Tuscan dialect. A bald man wearing Bermuda shorts recited the Our Father.

Nobody but nobody was looking at me.

"Do you want to see blood? Do you want me to do it? If you don't look at me, I swear I'll do it. Fuck, fucking look at me!"

Nobody was listening to me. I wiped my hand across my sweaty brow. That's when I saw the blood oozing on the white silk of my suit. Those people still in the room cried out, the man in the Bermuda shorts yelled, "Oh my God, she did it, she stuck that thing in her heart! Call an ambulance!" A pregnant woman fainted. The old lady from before looked like she was dead.

With my hand pressed against my dripping heart I cried, "Listen to me, I just want to talk!"

But they ran crying from the room. Nobody heard me.

I don't know in what damned language I spoke anyway.

Maybe the Italian tongue.

Maybe the Chinese tongue.

Maybe the tongue of looks.

Maybe the tongue of smiles.

Maybe Jimmy's tongue that he sweeps across my face.

Everyone had escaped now. Behind me, the Tuscan was furious: "You're fired, don't let me see you ever again." I hurried out. I called Livia Mega on my mobile.

The telephone was even more tired of life than I was. It died after the first ring. I opened my coat and lifted my shirt. I was still bleeding. I dabbed the tattoo with a tissue.

I took the flier for the photo exhibit out of my pocket, noted the address, and started running in that direction, towards the horrendous neighborhood where the show was being held in a university dorm.

Through the prison windows you could see the lanky shapes of brownnoses, future businessmen intently working on their laptops before a background of boring rock group posters. Then the kitchen. Then the common room. All full of people. A thousand open windows dumping their laughter whole on me.

I went in.

The first thing I saw, even before I saw my mother and Francis clinging to one another and swapping souls with their tongues, was the kingdom of azure that had its source in her dress and dove into the midnight blue of his suit.

It was a story with a happy ending that says, *Sky blue azure turquoise cobalt blue midnight blue navy.*

And then, *Prussian blue, steel blue, cornflower blue.*

And let's add, *Alice blue powder blue Persian blue.*

I could go on forever. There were all the blues that have ever existed and some that have never existed. Name one and you can bet it was there. My head was spinning. The longer I looked the more colors I found.

A protected marine park that began with sequins and ended with pinstripes.

Protecting the species known as beauty from people like me, I mean.

Mortifying them, people like me.

And that's precisely why those two were there, glued together, kissing, to mortify me with azure. To tell me with their tongues, but not with words, that I had no place there, none at all, and it didn't matter how I sacrificed myself for my mother, how I loved her. That has never mattered. It has never even mattered that I've lived, certainly not that I've survived. The only thing that matters to beauty is beauty itself, and everything else gets tossed into the wheelie bins on Christopher Road with the skinned carrion and the deformed clothes. For her it was not enough to be beautiful just once, she had to be female beauty multiplied by male beauty, blond by blond, tall times tall, a rifle of beauty, with two shots straight to my heart and nobody to pick up my corpse.

I took a step towards them.

Livia didn't look at me, not even out of the corner of her eye.

I took another step. In my tongue one says, "*soffrire come un cane*," to suffer like a dog. In dog tongue I don't know what they say. In Francis's tongue, well, his tongue was busy fishing around in Livia's mouth as if it wanted to haul her long-lost voice up from the depths of her throat.

She returned his attentions with her eyes closed and her right arm placed delicately on his waist, her fingers curved around him as if she were playing a long G on the flute.

Her sky blue Swarovski bracelet sent dancing flickers of light all around them like a fairy's spell.

Another step.

Persian blue, denim blue, aquamarine.

Yet another step.

She kept kissing him in that cursed blue painted blue. His ice-azure shirt emerged crystalline from the midnight blue of his coat. It occurred to me that if red stands for sex, then azure stands for the killer of the daughter who sacrificed herself for you. And, I thought, it appears that even filicide is performed as a couple.

I was standing in front of them now. Livia was caressing his hair slowly and respectfully as if she were polishing an Oscar but not once did she stop kissing him.

Who knows what it feels like to explore the tongue in that mouth that has ceased to fabricate meaning, that is now a mere mouth, a mouth for eating and kissing, a mouth consisting of palate, teeth, idle saliva and alveolus that the tongue no longer taps, and a soft palate whose posterior veil no longer makes "G"s and "K"s; it is just a veil now, one that if she wants she can wear at her fucking wedding.

The closer I got the more Livia's blond hair became an oracle of love dispensing propitious auguries of healthy, blond offspring.

The neon light on her head became a living illustration of that section in the American Declaration of Independence that talks about the right to the pursuit of happiness. Only at that point did I notice the photo behind them.

There was a bridge in the distance. Long dry branches in the foreground and far off, in the background, that bridge ready for night, its contours already known to the darkness, weak and blurry.

The stone forming long "M"s. Monster. Moribund.

It was Knaresborough Bridge.

"Mamma, I have to talk to you. Without him."

A look called *My-dearest-beloved* that, taking leave of his face, became *Ah it's you I'm curious to know what you think of the photos look at them up there.*

"I've been there, I've seen the bridge. I have to talk to you, please, listen to me."

Francis saying, "Oh, you've been there? Have you seen the castle?"

My mother pushing her hair behind her ears and happily watching the old couple that has just entered the room.

"Mamma, fuck, listen to me."

She walked over slowly to the two old people with their curved spines.

I turned to face my mother's five photos. They were all of Knaresborough Bridge. Two were taken from such a distance that the only thing separating the sky from the water was the line of black stone; another two had been taken from very close up and showed one of the fissures formed by the bridge and its reflection in the water, and inside that opening a hint of the houses on the opposite shore, light brown, checkered, all different sizes, all of them beautiful.

The last photo showed only the river with the reflection of the imposing towers. The water was black like a manhole cover, but you can bet that if you open it, and you dive in, it's like Pandora's box, and you're covered from head to foot in all of humankind's evils. Betrayal splatters all over your jacket, dishonesty goes up your nose, and hate straight into your eyes.

And on and on ad infinitum, or if you prefer until you die, evils splattered on every part of your body like Jimmy's sperm.

"Mamma, fuck, I have to talk to you. Let's go outside for a second!"

But she only had eyes for the two old people.

My mother came over to me and held me delicately by the wrist with her perfectly perfect hand, *So what do you think of the photos.* I felt the sweet softness of her palm. Isn't it incredible that that palm survived three years of hygienic abandon to land now, even softer and smoother and more impeccable than before, on my wrist? And isn't it monstrous that that reborn palm rested on him before it did on me?

I pulled my arm free and held her by the hand. My hand shook, it was damp. Her eyes popped open when I tightened my grip on her hand, then those tyrannical blue eyes asked me, *What is it dear?*

I gripped her even tighter. I moved her hand to my face and pushed her long fingers against my cheek on my tears. Her fingertips were like the bright keys of a flute.

She said the look, *You're hurting me.*

I returned the same look.

I sank my dirty chewed fingernails into the soft tissue between her baptism-white knuckles.

Livia Mega didn't move.

I felt her warm blood beneath my fingers.

She looked at me, expressionless.

I was crying harder now.

I cried for myself, drowned in Knaresborough River before my very eyes. And for Jimmy—who knew where he was happily performing his mission of insemination without me. And for Wen. And for Lily—who knew if she was alive? But then, who really is alive.

Once upon a time there were Sundays, and when they came my father stood in the still new, still spotless kitchen with his old leather bag on his shoulder and his Beatles notebook hanging around his neck. He'd tell me to drink my milk in a hurry because we had to go out, he had to rent one of Mizoguchi's masterpieces, and I swallowed the boiling liquid as fast as I could and said, "But don't tell me any stories, ok?"

My mother appeared in the kitchen wearing her white suit (she always dressed elegantly) and he'd say: "Who is it you're all dressed up for, eh?"

The wooden clock over the hot-plate ticked that it didn't give a damn if he treated her that way. Then I went outside. They argued. I watched the mouths on the other side of the glass spitting mute words.

She came out and gave me a weak kiss like those that ghosts give and then pointed her remote at her white Micra. I wanted to hug her.

I wanted to tell her that I adored her.

But I didn't move. I stood there venerating her telepathically.

Her Micra responded to the beep. She walked in slow motion, disciplined by her high heels. She got into her car. Then my father came out and closed the door behind him, saying, "Don't worry yourself about it, my little one, we're going to see a movie now, think about the beautiful story we're about to see, no?"

Livia Mega's face got whiter and whiter, as did her hands on my face, and she spoke several looks but I couldn't understand them. All of a sudden I was ignorant of the language of looks. I couldn't, I swear, I could no longer read the sheet music of her eyes.

All I could do was push my fingertips into her hands. My head was on fire, and I was sweating, my legs were shaking, and the people around me were lily-livered reflections on the waters of Knaresborough, and among them there was Francis with all his murderous beauty, right near me, and I moved away from her towards him. His face was angry, and he yelled something. I could no longer understand. My mother's man was leading me by the hand into another room and I was not resisting. He stopped for a second and waved Livia over. She was smiling like a child. My toes were being crushed in the shoes that were too big for me. It was a small room. There were some chairs, a notice board full of fliers about Jesus saving your life, and a soda machine.

Francis moved the chairs soundlessly and sat down. She sat down next to him, I sat down facing them. He stared at me wordlessly. He was wearing a blue tie with red and pale blue parrots on it.

We began playing a silent concert in ¾ time.

"On the flute, you won't be hearing Livia Mega. Stay with us on Pearl Radio."

Francis kept looking at me in no language.

There was something criminal about the fact that he made the same silence as my mother. I felt my gorge rising, blocking the words that I would have liked to say.

But surely in a short while he would stop looking at me, dirty with sweat and dressed in a suit that he had seen on a body much more beautiful than mine, and start talking.

Indeed, there was his voice now, saying, "I get it. You don't approve of my going out with your mother, but you'll have to get used to it. Things are becoming serious between us."

And my mother smiling a smile that said nothing to me.

And me: "How long have you been going out together?"

She persisted with her speechless smile, he followed her lead, like they were competing to see who had the most beautiful teeth. For that matter, when did her teeth turn so fucking white again? And where was I when all this happened?

I pleaded with a gaze called *Mamma answer me why haven't you said a word to me since you met him?*

Francis caressed Livia's shoulder and said, "Camelia, can't you see how your mother is smiling at you? Go on, before it gets dark, go have fun with your friends?"

Outside a storm was raging. The sky was the color of my keyboard stripped of keys. Sheets of dirty rain slobbered all over the Leeds-gray façade of the student housing building. It looked as if the concrete itself was being melted away by acid, and the windows closed in quick succession as if choreographed. The last brownnose shut his laptop. The last bulimic turned the light off in the kitchen. The last socialite closed the door of the common room. The last pigeon flew off the last balcony, then was struck by lightning and fell. My head was throbbing and I felt menacing movements in my stomach. I took a step, then another. My pants dragged mud, used tissues, and phosphorescent condoms behind me.

I inhaled and exhaled.

The pigeon could still move its head. But the rain was slowly decanting its intestines down the drain.

To my left, the final open convenience store chased the last customer out. I stopped him and asked him what time it was.

"Sorry, I don't have a watch."

"Do you know what day it is?"

"Sorry?"

"I said, what day . . . "

I vomited the word "day" on the wet asphalt, first in English, then in Italian, and finally in Chinese.

The kid ran off as if I were spitting nuclear poison. I gazed at the vaguely ideographic filaments of my vomit. The rain fell in perfect spirals on the green vomit and turned it from a mulch green to a forest green with a hint of dark gray. Loose pieces of battered fish moved around, pushed this way and that by the rills of water, and made their way to the wrappers bobbing around in the gutter. A candy wrapper ended up in the drain; another containing whole peanuts stayed on top to be trammeled by the rain. I opened my umbrella. The wind instantly whipped it out of my hands and dumped it in the puddle of vomit.

People walked serenely by, dressed in shorts. Some were laughing. Two hundred ants ferried across the puddle on my shoes and then dove off, one after another, into the organic Disneyland of the pigeon's innards. The umbrella spun around in my vomit.

Key for umbrella? For vomit? For ant? For an ugly girl who should just put an end to it? What do I know, what the hell do I know?

My mobile beeped. It was a text from Jimmy.

An infinite series of empty squares.

I replied: "Tell me, Jimmy, I'm here, but tell me in English because my mobile can't read ideograms."

Him: "Yes, I know. I just got the number wrong."

I started running.

The rain got heavier. There was lightning and thunder and, well, anything else you care to name. Say blinding flashes of lightning like spotlights shining on the stage of my disastrous life. Say plague of locusts. Say cyanide rain. Say you'll write "she should have died sooner" on my grave.

I got to Wen's shop. The rain fell in cudgels, pounding my brain. I went in and slammed the door behind me. The red cat jumped, and belted out its annoying ding-dong.

"Camelia, what happened to you? Are you hurt?"

"I'm going to kill you if you don't tell me everything."

I pulled up my shirt.

"Ah, it's a tattoo. Why that ideogram?"

"Because it's mine. I invented it."

"Listen, it exists, you know?"

"Wen, was Lily with you or with Jimmy? Were you in love with her? Did you reject her like you did me and so she started screwing Jimmy?"

He walked closer to me and I pushed him to the ground. It was so easy, he was as light as a toy. From the floor he looked up at me through wide eyes, his breathing hard.

"Do you want me to kill you? I will if you don't tell me everything."

"I love you. I loved her, too. You both seemed so happy with me, but then you both went with my brother."

"Fuck, why did you say no to us? Are you crazy or something? Are you sick in the head?"

"I said no because . . . "

Silence. I lifted my enormous shoe up over his little porcelain hand on the floor.

"So?"

"So, forgive me but it's not my fault."

My foot came closer to his fingers. "What?" I said.

He cried.

"I can't make love, I can't."

"What do you mean? You're . . . impotent?"

"I don't know. I think so."

I stepped away from him. He stood up. So as not to die of suffocation I examined, one by one, the three sleeveless shirts hanging in a row behind him. The sequence of buttons.

"Wen, is Lily dead?"

He bit his fingernails, inhaled and exhaled. "She threw herself off Knaresborough Bridge," he said. "Ah, and your tattoo means 'hole.'"

He opened the red door and disappeared forever.

The next day I was woken by a strange smell. Food. Not food past its best before date or unrecognizable beneath kilos of mold. Not symbolic food like Morrisons' canned meatballs. Not even frozen food, or food stolen from the footless beggar by Christopher Road kids. Real food. God-given real food. Grown, not created. I went down the stairs, my mother was on her knees with her head in the oven.

It can't be.

The only use our oven had ever had was as a set for my imagined suicide. In those fantasies it was my head stuffed inside, not hers; my skin separated from my body like the morsels of meat at the tattoo parlor. But now, there was my mother pulling away from the oven with her perfect face. She was wearing a white and pink apron with two cows hugging and in her hands she held a tray of impeccable lasagna.

It can't be.

"Mamma, but . . . "

Her smile began as a greeting to me but immediately became a declaration of love for her man.

He was there, sitting at the table, wearing the same suit as the day before. Blue declined into all its possibilities, the bright parrots of his tie. His splendid eyes and the sublime profile of his nose.

The minute he saw me he moved his hand slightly and smiled. That movement unleashed a long shimmering light that moved over his entire pinstriped suit as if refracted through water. Between that light and me there was half a staircase and an entire universe.

Livia filled his plate and then her own.

She sat down at the table.

Our table. Our lurid, rotten table, honored guest at meals that were more like vomit-soaked survival tests; our naked table, stripped to its raw cheap wood, stained with sauces of every color and assorted bodily fluids.

Our table full of holes.

Our table that fires off Gatling gun bursts of nuclear memories: Livia Mega sitting in her lingerie with her eyes half closed, a Polaroid camera on her chest in place of her heart.

Our table was now masquerading as a normal table belonging to a normal family. It was dressed in a tablecloth. Blue with obese cherries and a border of obese strawberries. And on the table two china plates, not plastic ones, arching upwards like real soup plates, like angels in a crèche.

Our table was set for two.

"Mamma, why didn't you set a place for me?"

And her gaze that began with *You were sleeping so soundly* and quickly became *Do you like them honey?*

They ate and smiled. I stood on the stairs. I breathed in and blew out. I heard their teeth chewing my body and swallowing. I dug my fingernails into the palms of my hands. With his mouth full, he said, "Mmm," and, "Can you pass me the pepper, sweetheart?"

In the middle of the table, right over the hole, there was a blue vase regurgitating fat heads of orchids. How they didn't topple over was a mystery. They emitted a terrorist fragrance that was impossible to ignore, that bypassed the mucous membranes and went straight to your brain. I came down the stairs and opened the oven.

The baking pan was empty.

"But you didn't leave any for me . . . "

Livia Mega turned her head and spoke a gaze called *Next time I promise!*

Then she dispatched a smile like a Christmas card destined for someone you never visit.

"You know, honey," he said, "you're a fantastic cook."

I clenched my fists. My fingers were tipped with blood.

At that moment I noticed that next to the stove, in pieces, was my mother's flute. The three pieces were in a row between the bag of sugar and the empty egg carton.

"Mamma, what's your flute doing there in the middle of all that food?"

"Your mother just taught me how to play a couple of notes."

I picked up the longest piece, the one with sixteen keys. I looked inside it like I did when I was a kid, turning it around as if it were a kaleidoscope. The light swirled and created strange forms and fell into the grooves of the keys. I imagined myself running inside as if it were a tube that led me to my mother, like if I got to the end without falling into one of the holes she would hug me.

I turned to look at her straight back. I watched her as she brought the fork to her mouth. Her extraordinary profile. Her bright, washed hair. Francis across the table from her eating and smiling.

The living sound of the silverware.

I picked up the head of the flute, the piece with the oval hole for her splendid lips. When I looked inside I was shocked to discover my own eye there. I inserted the longer piece into the head.

I looked inside again.

The reflection of my eye had disappeared. There was nothing but a black hole.

Francis: "Camelia, do you know how to play, too?"

"No."

"Your mother taught me how to play the simplest note, G. You must know how to play that at least."

Livia turned to look at me. She put the fork down.

I attached the third piece to the other two and lifted the flute to my lips. I pushed down with the index finger of my left hand and the little finger of my right hand on the keys corresponding to the note G. I blew.

The sound of balloons bursting in the distance. Nothing else.

Francis smiled compassionately.

My mother too.

Francis looked at her and said, "Do you want to marry me, Livia?"

I held my breath.

Her fork suspended in midair, she opened her mouth.

Not to fill it with lasagna.

Not to kiss him.

A sound came from the mouth of Livia Mega.

A meaning.

A real word.

A "yes."

I dropped the flute.

It tumbled over to Francis, who was smiling happily. He picked it up. He said: "Camelia, you have to be careful with beautiful things."

I left the house.

Francis said: "Have fun, love."

His future wife did not run after me. I closed the door behind me, and stood motionless in the middle of the wet street.

The mute houses of Christopher Road, as if suddenly waking from their hibernation, now reverberated with words. Old words, words belonging to babies, to adults, to deaf-and-dumb mutes, to dogs and cats, to parrots, to talking iguanas, to dolls when you press their bellies, to plasma TVs, to Gagliardi washing machines. Shouts and whispers and murmurs and songs. A veritable rapture of sounds riddled with meanings. Meanings that had nothing to do with me.

I tried convincing my nostrils that they should allow a bit of oxygen in. It was difficult, difficult, impossible to stay on my feet. A high-pitched sound came from the wheelie to my right. I lifted the lid shakily. Two white shirts with six sleeves were rocking to the rhythm of the sounds. I lifted one up.

Two beautiful white and orange cats were having sex. They didn't look like feral cats. When the male saw me he removed himself from her and turned a yellow-blue look full of hatred on me. His tail went straight. He made a threatening sound.

But I couldn't help myself. I stretched out my arms to that stupendous coat of fur. I touched it. He bit me. Blood. I started running without any idea of where I would stop. A race in which if you stop you are punished with immortality. The Africans in Number 6 were repainting their house green. They talked and talked and laughed. Two kids were kissing on the corner, the girl had splendid red hair that stretched down to her ankles. Every now and again I turned left or right, or closed my eyes, daring the light poles to block my way, or I stopped to find out if I was still breathing. At some point, exhausted, I fell onto the sidewalk. Nobody stopped to ask how I was.

I got up and kept running until I reached the wall of forbidden beauty. I looked around. Nobody was there.

There was a brick sticking out and I put my foot on it and started to climb. For some reason I was convinced that it was the most intelligent thing to do. I told myself I had to make it. That if I didn't get to the top I would die. No, wait, even worse: if I didn't get to the top I would not die.

I pulled myself up with all my strength and made it all the way up. I sat on the top of the wall. Those houses that to me had always been nothing more than demos, a sampling of pitched roofs and brown bricks, and lively chimneys that wrote poetry in smoke on a sky that was bluer than mine, were now real houses with real people going in and out of them.

That revelation of human life in the middle of something beautiful had something vaguely morbid about it. It was like a scene from a science fiction movie. I looked around at the plants: they were normal height and color and real people were watering them. I looked at the cars moving.

I was so tired. I slipped my shoes off. They fell to the ground with a dull thud. In just a few hours they had dramatically deformed my feet, as if I had been wearing stones on my feet, like they did in ancient China.

Only then did I realize that the street I was looking at was none other than Grosvenor Road.

My mobile phone rang.

"Hi Camelia, it's Francis."

Even distorted by the phone his fucking voice was stupendous. Listen, your mother and I are going to York, to my apartment for a few days. Tell me where you are so I can bring you the keys to your place."

" . . . "

"Hello, Camelia. Are you there?"

"And where do I go while you're in York?"

"What? Aren't you old enough to stay at home by yourself? Listen, tell me where you are?

" . . . "

"Camelia, can you hear me? Hello?"

"Grosvenor Road."

"Ah, ok, nearby, I'm on my way. Whereabouts on Grosvenor Road?"

" . . . "

"Are you there? Have a look at the house number."

"No."

"No, what? You can't see any? Ah, are you somewhere near the residence?"

"No."

"Okay, listen, I'm coming. I'll see you in a bit—"

I hung up. I'd had enough. My vision was fuzzy and my head ached. The plants and the people were luminous blurs. And why was it still light? What happened to the night? What time is it? What day is it? My gorge rose and sank, rose and sank. I could feel only that which in my body was hurting. I touched the wounds on my legs. They were still there. Then the tattoo. Then my pocket. In my pocket I found the little knife and pulled it out.

I caressed the blade with two fingers. It was cold. Smooth. Shiny. It was finally time.

There was a sky above my head. It was washbasin white, that color to which Leeds has subscribed, and every twenty skies like this it wins an airplane disaster. It was that white that promises snow, and like every promise that can be trusted it swore on somebody's grave to keep it.

I ran my fingers up and down the blade. How hard can it

really be? It's over in a second. Push the blade into your throat, like jewels placed in my mother's safe, like when she would say, "One day this will be yours."

I felt my heart beating like mad in my fingertips. Boom. Then, boom. And again, boom. Then—

"There you are! Here are the keys."

Francis was standing at the bottom of the wall, right below me, still with his suicide good looks, still handsome enough to be stopped by the police for exceeding the beauty limit.

"What do you have in your hand, Camelia? Oh God, are you crazy? I won't allow you to hurt yourself, come down from there."

"It's my life."

"No, listen, wait, whatever it is that is making you sad, know that—"

"Don't think you can fucking stop me."

"Come down!"

His aura was so strong it hurt your eyes. He seemed to be light-years away. The parrots flashed a harsh silken light. My fingers trembled, they were damp with sweat. A cold, slimy sweat like snail muck. I clenched the handle as hard as I could.

"If you don't come down then I'm coming up."

He put a blue foot on a brick, pushed himself up to the next protruding brick, and then he was up, sitting to my left. He put his arm around my neck. The fabric of his suit was terribly soft. I couldn't breathe.

"Listen, Camelia. Listen."

"You're the one who doesn't listen to me."

"No, listen, everything passes, give me that thing, come on, use your head."

"Why are you going to York?"

"What's wrong with that? It's just for a couple of days. I mean, once we're married, maybe we'll go there to live, but right now it's just for the weekend, Camy."

I raised the knife, he jumped and extended his splendid pianist's hand toward me, toward my right hand, which wouldn't release its grip.

"Give it to me, Camelia."

He leaned towards me and grabbed my wrist, balancing himself with his left hand on the wall. I had my feet on a little ledge and didn't need to lean my hands on the wall. He reached out for the knife again, I let go, and he grabbed it. Right at that moment, as he was leaning toward me, as his fingers closed around the handle of the knife, I saw my left hand push him hard.

He fell, headfirst. I watched him until I could breathe again. I watched the blood spread.

Whether you see me or not, I'm the one with the black hair and the buy-one-get-three nose. That one there, where it is night already, where it's all over, even if you wanted a story where everything sounds right, where everything is the right color, and there are butterflies flying and people who talk and love and talk and love.

You can get away with a story like that. You can fuck a story like that all night and have yourself another one, and then another, until you fill your life with butterflies and memories that don't fade. Well, you know what I say? Use it to mop the bathroom, that story of yours, or I don't know, to line the hamster's cage. Whatever, just make sure you get it out of the way, because here in Leeds you won't need it, and if you take it out here, the Christopher Road kids will kill it.

Livia Mega was sitting in front of the TV. She was wearing an indigo outfit and a long amethyst necklace. A complicated blond braid hung down over her breast like a gold medal.

She was watching the Icelandic movie—who knows how long the DVD had been in the house. It was the scene where, following the fatal avalanche, Nói is sitting on the snow looking into a pair of toy binoculars. He sees images of palm trees and sun kissed beaches.

Then she saw me. She spoke, using words: "You don't know where Francis went after he gave you the keys, do you? He was supposed to pick me up three hours ago . . . We've missed the train by now."

I replied with the smile *Everything's okay mamma.*

I closed the door.

She stood up, and came over to me. She looked at the tie with the parrots that I was wearing around my waist. She stepped backwards, her hand over her mouth, and didn't say a single look. I felt wind in my ear.

"Don't worry, Mamma. Everything is going to be like it was before. We're alone again. Forever. Like I promised you."

I turned to the open window. It was snowing, even though it was already the twelfth. Of which month, I couldn't say. I shut the window.

ABOUT THE AUTHOR

Viola Di Grado was born in Catania, Italy.
70% Acrylic 30% Wool, winner of the 2011
Campiello First Novel Award and a finalist
for Italy's most prestigious literary prize, the
Strega, is her first book.